3/17
BTL
KT-179-978

"Gripping . . . how often can we honestly say that a book is unlike anything else? Yet here it is, unique in form and effect . . . Nors has found a novel way of getting into the human heart"

Guardian

"To read a Dorthe Nors story is to enter a dream and become subject to its logic . . . Nors knows and understands so much about us; her perceptions frequently shock with their acuity, though within seconds you recognize them as, yes, true"

Daniel Woodrell, award-winning author of *Winter's Bone*

"Unsettling and poetic . . . Some pieces . . . are oddly beautiful; others are brilliantly disturbing"

The New York Times

"Nors's prose is direct . . . a series of uncluttered and voice-driven sentences that achieve their rhythm through careful juxtaposition and build"

Chicago Tribune

"The intricately crafted stories in *Karate Chop*, from popular Danish writer Dorthe Nors, focus on ordinary occurrences . . . and then twist them into brilliantly slanted cautionary tales about desire, romance, deception, and dread"

Elle

"Nors has found her own space away from Copenhagen's literati . . . Her words whip along, each idea cascading into the next: it's like having a window into someone's thoughts"

Independent

"Darkly funny and incisive . . . In these literary body-blows, Nors takes merciless aim at families, relationships and egos"

Times

9030 00005 3995 3

"Dorthe Nors's story collection, *Karate Chop*, also blew me away . . . these are some of the best five-page stories I've ever read"

Irish Times

"Nors has a great knack . . . for portraying the voids and fault lines in an unbalanced mind . . . crisp, quirky, jarringly funny"

Times Literary Supplement

"My favorite discovery was *Minna Needs Rehearsal Space* by the ferociously-talented Danish writer Dorthe Nors . . . a beautiful, moving, totally compelling account of one woman's yearning. I simply can't wait for Nors's next English translation"

The Herald

"The short-short stories in Danish sensation Nors's slim, potent collection . . . evoke the weirdness and wonder of relating in the digital age"

Vogue

"Spare and sublime. Dorthe Nors knows how to capture the smallest moments and sculpt them into the unforgettable"

Oprah Magazine

"Dorthe Nors is a writer of moments—quiet, raw portraits of existential meditation, at times dyspeptic, but never unsympathetic"

Paris Review

"In this slim collection of stories, the Danish Nors examines everyday issues with intensity and force"

Marie Claire

"Beautiful, faceted, haunting storics . . . a rising star of Danish letters"

Junot Diaz, author of *This Is How You Lose Her*

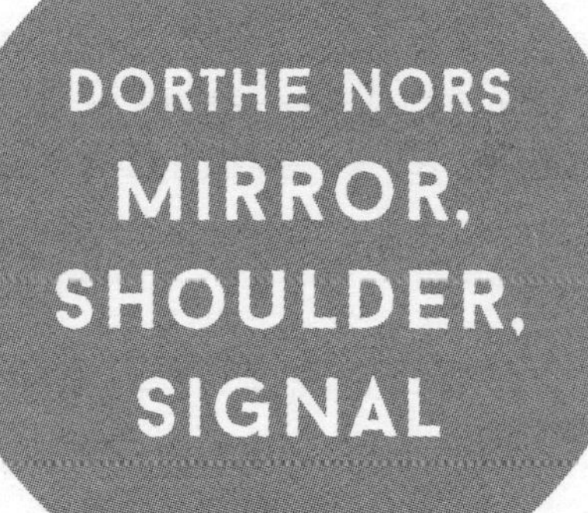

Translated from the Danish
by **MISHA HOEKSTRA**

PUSHKIN PRESS

Pushkin Press
71–75 Shelton Street
London WC2H 9JQ

Original text © 2016 Dorthe Nors. Published by agreement with Ahlander Agency

Mirror, Shoulder, Signal was first published as *Spejl, skulder, blink* in Denmark in 2016

English translation © 2017 Misha Hoekstra

First published by Pushkin Press in 2017

1 3 5 7 9 8 6 4 2

ISBN 978 1 782273 12 7

DANISH ARTS FOUNDATION

Grateful acknowledgment is made to the Danish Arts Foundation for supporting the writing and translation of this book. Thank you also to Copydan for additional translation support awarded through Autorkontoen by the Danish Authors' Society, and to Hald Hovedgaard for a translation residency.

Every effort has been made to trace copyright holders and to obtain their permission for the use of copyright material. If you are aware of any errors or omissions the publisher will endeavour to incorporate amendments in future reprints.

All rights reserved. No part of this publication may be reproduced, stored in a retrieval system or transmitted in any form or by any means, electronic, mechanical, photocopying, recording or otherwise, without prior permission in writing from Pushkin Press

"You take the straight way from Earth to Heaven" translated from the Danish "Velkommen, Lærkelil!" ("Welcome, Little Lark!") by Christian Richardt, in *Texter og Toner, Bind I: Blandede Digte*, 1868. Various lines of dialog from the film *Contact*, 1997. "And life is brief, so brief…" translated from the Danish "Heksedansen", 1960, itself a translation by Peter Mynte of the Norwegian song of the same title and same year by Vidar Sandbeck.

Set in Monotype Baskerville by Tetragon, London
Printed and bound by CPI Group (UK) Ltd, Croydon, CRO 4YY

www.pushkinpress.com

LONDON BOROUGH OF WANDSWORTH	
9030 00005 3995 3	
Askews & Holts	23-Feb-2017
AF	£10.99
	WW16018826

1.

SONJA IS SITTING IN A CAR, and she's brought her dictionary along. It's heavy, and sits in the bag on the backseat. She's halfway through her translation of Gösta Svensson's latest crime novel, and the quality was already dipping with the previous one. *Now's the time I can afford it*, she thought, and so she looked for driving schools online and signed up with Folke in Frederiksberg. The theory classroom was small and blue and reeked of stale smoke and locker rooms, but the theory itself went well. Besides Folke, there was only one other person Sonja's age in the class, and he was there because of drunk driving, so he kept to himself. Sonja usually sat there and stuck out among all the kids, and for the first aid unit the instructor used her as a model. He pointed to the spot on her throat where they were supposed to imagine her breathing had gotten blocked. He did the Heimlich on her, his fingers up in her face, inside her collar, up and down her arms. At one point he put her into a stranglehold, but that wasn't the worst of it. The worst was when they had to do the exercises themselves. It was humiliating to be placed in the recovery position by a boy of eighteen. It also made her dizzy, and that was something no one was supposed to find out.

"You're such a fighter," her mom always said, and Sonja is a fighter; she doesn't give up. She ought to, but she doesn't. "And then you compress the heart hard thirty times and pay attention to whether they're breathing," the first aid instructor said.

That's all that counts in the end, Sonja had thought, *breathing*, and she passed theory. With her the problem's always practice, which is why she's now sitting in a car. It's great that she's made it this far, even if it's not far enough; she just wishes she were skilled and experienced. Like Sonja's sister Kate and Kate's husband Frank, who got their licenses in the eighties. Back home in Balling, folks were driving souped-up pickups, burning rubber, off-roading. All those accidents the adult Kate fears now are things she'd gloried in as a teen. She'd been a stowaway in rolling wrecks, a barn-dance femme fatale, and the belle of clubs and gym meets. It wouldn't surprise Sonja to learn that Kate used to sneak the car home the back way. In Balling, cars would slink along the road behind the church, and Sonja's car tiptoes around too, but that's because she's a terrible driver. The car as mechanism is hard for her to fathom, and her driving lessons have been plagued with problems. The biggest of them is sitting in the car right now, next to Sonja. Her name is Jytte, and it's her smoke that clings to the theory classroom. Surfaces at the driving school are galvanized with cigarette smoke, and most of it took a trip through Jytte's lungs first. When Sonja arrives at the school, Jytte's sitting in Folke's office, on Facebook or going through other students' medical records. "Melanie with the ponytail wasn't certified by the doctor!" she shouts over to

Sonja in the doorway. "Something wrong with her nerves, did you know that?"

Sonja didn't know, and she hasn't been certified by the medical officer either. She's got an ear disorder. It's an inherited condition from her mother's side; none of them can maintain their balance when their heads are in certain positions. For a long time she thought she'd escaped it, but then it showed up, the positional dizziness. It's called benign paroxysmal positional vertigo, but that's far too much Latin for the place Sonja comes from. And besides, she's got it under control. It's not going to keep her from doing squat, and so now she's sitting in the car. She's got Gösta in the backseat, and Jytte at her side.

Because Jytte's got a lot on her mind, she hasn't had time to teach Sonja to shift for herself. Sonja's been driving with Jytte for six months, and still she fumbles with the gears. Jytte seizes the initiative and deals with it for her, since when Jytte deals with changing gears, there's no need for her to change topics: her son's getting married, her grandkid's going to be called something ghastly, the fiancée's got a cockamamie clothing sense, and the sister of her brother-in-law's mother's new husband just died.

"Thai people just can't drive."

Sonja and Jytte are in Frederiksberg, waiting for a traffic light. Smoke from the last cigarette out the window has been sucked into the passenger compartment, and it mixes with the sweat that Sonja excretes. She signals right, Jytte's hand on the gearstick, and keeps an eye out for cyclists.

"This woman I've got now is called Pakpao. Pakpao!? GREEN LIGHT! SECOND GEAR, SECOND GEAR, BIKE!"

Jytte shifts to second while Sonja swerves to miss the bike.

"And then she's married to this dirty old man who's seventy-five. He's been down in the office, completely bloated and all."

They've gone a fair piece toward the inner city and traffic is light, so Jytte can shift to fourth no problem. She uses the passenger-side clutch and then points at a deli.

"They make a good headcheese in there, and this warm liver pâté with bacon and cocktail wieners. I *love* Christmas, I simply can't get enough of it. Don't you just love Christmas?"

It's early August, and Sonja does not like Christmas. It all revolves around Kate's shopping lists and minimizing damage by winding back time, and yet she nods anyway. She wants to stay on Jytte's good side since in truth, it's Jytte who's driving the car. Actually, Sonja has a soft spot for her, because Jytte's told her that she comes from the Djursland peninsula. From a small village in the direction of Nimtofte. Jytte's father ran the local feed store, right across from school, so Jytte could run home and eat during lunch hour. She moved to Copenhagen when she was twenty. The village constable had a younger brother with an extra room in the suburb of Hvidovre. He was a cop himself, the younger brother, and Jytte's always had a weakness for a man in uniform. Now she lives inland, in Solrød, but back then the thing was to go out dancing till you no longer stank of Danish farmland.

Sonja's told Jytte she has a hard time believing that Jytte's also from Jutland. Sonja can't hear it in her speech, and in general she has a hard time understanding what Jytte's saying. Turn left is *turleff*, turn right *trite*, and it's not really dialect to speak of. It's just the fastest way for Jytte to bark commands without changing topics.

"There's not much Jutland left in you," Sonja says now.

"You should just hear—trite—when I talk on the phone to my sister. GREEN ARROW, GREEN ARROW, TURN GOD-DAMMIT, BIKE!"

Sonja turns right and thinks about how she herself might sound when she talks on the phone to Kate. But she hardly every talks to Kate anymore, and now they're headed toward the Vesterbro quarter. Ahead of them lies Istedgade, with its traffic quagmire, and Jytte is saying that she likes Swedish stair-step candles to be in the windows. There should also be tinsel on the Christmas tree, but that's not the way her son's fiancée sees it. At *her* place, the tree always has to be trimmed in white, and Jytte just doesn't get it, just like she doesn't get why Folke lets so many foreigners into the driving school.

"They can go to their own driving schools," Jytte says. "They can't understand what I say. I—turleff—take my life in my hands every time I drive with them."

Sonja thinks about the feed store in Djursland. Back home in Balling, they had one of them too. Across the road lay a grocery store, known as Super Aage's on account of the manager's first name. Now there's no grocer, no butcher, no post office in Balling. The farms have swallowed each other up so only two are left, and they've taken out all the dairy cart tracks, the gossip paths, the old sunken roads. Balling lies like an isolated instance of civilization in an oversized cornfield, though out past that, the heath has escaped the drive for efficiency. There are whooper swans there, and while almost no one farms anymore, farmhouse kitchens are still huge—the size of small cafeterias. A long laminated table at one end for the vanished farmhands, and then the modern cabinets by the window. You always had to scoot over on the bench when they came in to eat, and then there's Jytte, sitting in Djursland, dangling her legs. It's the lunch hour, she's run home to eat, and her feet don't reach the floor. She's wearing red bobby sox and a plaid skirt. Her mother's placed a slice of white bread before her. Her mother bakes the bread herself; it's dry, and Jytte spreads margarine on it. Then she grabs the package of brown sugar. It makes a crunching sound. It's fun pressing the brown sugar into the margarine. She can spend a long time pressing it in. Afterward, she listens to how the brown sugar keeps crunching in her mouth. It dissolves in her spit, which becomes sweet, like syrup. The bell's going to ring soon. When it rings, her mother yells that she's going to be late. Jytte's forced to run across the road, her legs going like drumsticks.

"BRAKE GODDAMMIT! CAN'T YOU FUCKING SEE THE CROSSWALK?"

Jytte's stomped on the brake and clutch. They're stopped at a pedestrian crossing, staring at a frightened man in a windbreaker.

"You have to stop for people!" Jytte says.

"I know that," Sonja says.

"It doesn't fucking look that way!" Jytte says, and she releases the clutch, first, second.

Jytte's phone rings. They pass Vesterbrogade, third gear. Jytte's husband has mornings off, and he can't find the remote.

"IT'S IN THE BASKET. YEAH, THE BASKET BESIDE THE—trite, signal, signal goddammit, turleff, slowly, slowly!— . . . PORK RIB ROAST, I THINK."

They drive up Istedgade amid glistening shoals of bikes. Sonja's vision is a fog and she almost can't breathe, yet at the intersection by Enghavevej she manages a left turn pretty much on her own. Jytte's no longer talking to her husband, but she's discovered a text with a photo from her son's fiancée. It depicts her grandchild in a christening dress and Jytte's voice grows elastic, for Sonja has to see the picture too, but Sonja would prefer to wait if she may, and then Jytte places the phone up on the dashboard.

It's difficult to maintain boundaries in an automobile. When you're a driving student, you have to relinquish free will, and once Jytte forced her to overtake a hot dog cart. They'd been driving around calmly enough, but then they'd come to a place where there was a traffic island on the street. A traffic island and a hot dog cart that was creeping forward. Sonja wasn't supposed to pass, but people in back became impatient and started honking. "Pass, God damn you, pass!" yelled Jytte, whereupon Sonja crossed over into the lane of oncoming traffic, passed, and then turned back into her own lane so quickly that she nearly clipped the hot dog man. He was walking along in front, of course, hauling the cart. "You almost had his blood on your hands there," Jytte said.

That still lingers in her body as shame. Shame, and fear of manslaughter, and now they're approaching Vigerslev Boulevard. The road goes past Western Cemetery, and Jytte decides they're going to turn and drive the entire way around it.

"You know, I really like Western Cemetery," Sonja says, trying to make conversation. "Down in the bottom part is a chapel with plywood over the windows. I think they've stopped using it. There's this avenue of gnarled old poplars there too. And a pond. I love to take a blanket and lie there and read."

To Jytte, reading is for people on holiday, and cemeteries are for the dead. In Jytte's family, the dead are numerous. Some have been killed in traffic accidents, others have died from cancer or workplace accidents. Her mother's still alive, but her sister has lung disease, and then Sonja should turn. She should turn left. Mirror, shoulder, signal, and in with the clutch. Jytte downshifts to second, but Sonja gets to pick the lane herself. She picks the correct one, which isn't so easy when there are so many. The light's red and they're sitting there in first gear, waiting. In the lane to their right is a delivery van, revving its engine.

"Aborigines," Jytte says, pointing at the van.

Sonja looks up at the traffic signal. The light changes. She lets out the clutch and drives forward. So does the van, and then it starts turning in front of Sonja. It's against the law to make a left turn from a right lane. Sonja knows that, and so does Jytte. Jytte's already rolled down her window, and one hand is out the window with middle finger extended, the other hand over by the steering wheel to honk the horn. She gives them horn and finger, and the car stops in the intersection in the middle of a green light. The van has stopped too, and now its driver window rolls down.

"CHINKS!" shouts Jytte.

"FUCKING *HO*!" shouts the driver.

Sonja thinks about the dead prime ministers in the cemetery. It's lovely to take a blanket there. Then she can lie on it, looking at Hans Hedtoft while the ducks quack and the roof of the big chapel gleams in the sun. It's like the New Jerusalem, or a little patch of far-off Denmark. The sound of cars in the distance, the scent of yew and boxwood; almost the middle of nowhere. In theory a stag might drift past, and she's bought a cookie for her coffee, pilfered some ivy from the undergrowth. The dead make no noise, and if she's lucky a bird of prey might soar overhead. Then she'll lie there, and escape.

2.

"THERE'S SOME TROUBLE with my neck and arms," Sonja says.

It's Thursday, and the air hangs heavy and close. She's lying on the massage table with her head down in the mini bathing ring. Her jaw tenses against the leather; it ached when she brushed her teeth. It's as if the joint's rusted, although right now her masseuse is working on her butt. A little while later, she works her way up and says that something's wandered from Sonja's abdomen, up through her body. Anger, most likely. And it's on the cusp of wanting to come out her mouth. She should just let it out, says the masseuse, whose name is Ellen.

"Out with it," she says.

In the room that serves as massage clinic, the floorboards are all planed. The places where branches once sat on the trunk are demarcated clearly. The bedroom belonging to Sonja's parents had been paneled in wood, and there were knotholes everywhere. While her mother read a tabloid, and her father rustled his newspaper, Sonja would lay there and set the wood surfaces in motion. She could get a knot to look like many things: birds, automobiles, the characters in *Donald Duck*. The floor at Ellen's is alive in the same way, and now she's got a good grip on Sonja's butt cheek. She says that Sonja keeps tensing up, and when Sonja got there twenty minutes ago, the door stood ajar to Ellen's kitchen. Sonja tried to peer inside but didn't manage to see anything other than some knitting on the counter. She doesn't know much about Ellen, except that she's good at massage and there's something wistful in her eyes.

"Your buttocks are hard," Ellen says. "That's because, if you'll pardon a vulgar phrase, you're a tight-ass with your feelings. An emotional tight-ass, a tight-fisted tightwad. Can't you hear how everything's right there in the words?"

With the job Sonja has, that's something she knows quite well. Language is powerful, almost magic, and the smallest alteration can elevate a sentence or be its undoing.

"I think you should ask for more calm when you're in the car."

Driving school problems are a recurring theme at the clinic, and Ellen's advice is always confrontation. But Sonja gave up on asking for calm long ago. There's no way it would pay off. If Sonja requested calm, Jytte might try, all right, but it wouldn't last long. Just being dictated to by a student like that would play havoc with Jytte's mind. With Jytte, all bad things stem from quiet. Just like Kate, Jytte senses danger in blank expanses, so the thing is to abrade them with tedious speech, cake recipes, dog hair.

Ellen's hands have a good grip on Sonja, and it's far too seldom that Sonja puts herself in someone else's hands. She imagines that Ellen's hands are stronger than most. Ellen carries a lot of stuff around, and it's not likely that all her clients can get up on the table by themselves. "Everyone needs to be met in their body," Ellen likes to say, and Kate has strong hands too. At the nursing home where she works, they have hoists for the elderly and infirm. Yet she still can't avoid lifting people, and both she and Ellen are strong that way, and now Ellen's moved from Sonja's buttocks to the back of her heart.

The back of the heart is the spot between the shoulder blades. Ellen calls it the back of the heart because that's where you get stabbed when you get stabbed in the back. The spot is tender in Sonja. So tender that she stares hard at a knot on the floor while Ellen rubs. The knot resembles Mickey Mouse with his ears a bit too large, and he's standing with his hands at his side. He's got gloves on his hands and yellow buttons on his pants, he's calling for Pluto and the dog's supposed to come, he's supposed to come *now*. It's painful, and her upper arms hurt too; they feel like big bruises.

"Oh jeez," Sonja says, "there too."

"Why do you think your arms are so sore?"

Sonja says it might be because she was in this brawl in an intersection by Western Cemetery. She thought she'd told Ellen already during her other lament about Jytte, but apparently she hadn't. It feels good to say it now, and she also tells Ellen about how it had been on the drive back to Folke's Driving School. How Jytte had gotten rather huffy. At one point, Sonja tried to shift gears herself, and she shouldn't have done that, because then Jytte accused her of trying to destroy the car.

"I was ready to cry," Sonja says.

Ellen places her warm hands on Sonja's upper arms.

"That was pretty unfair."

Sonja can feel the muscles in her right upper arm relax a little. It's Ellen's hands, they're patting her, and the fingers are massaging a spot behind her ear, and Sonja's a woman in the middle of her life, she's an adult now. She no longer needs for people to always get along, and she can't make them either. They're not very accepting, they won't open up. Kate, for instance, doesn't answer the phone anymore.

"Ready for the other side?" Ellen asks, and Sonja tries to nod.

It isn't easy with her head in the bathing ring, and flipping over can be tricky besides; certain angles trigger the positional vertigo. Having her head in the so-called dentist position is awful. According to Ellen, Sonja's dizziness is an expression of a spiritual condition, and Sonja's explained that in that case, it's a spiritual condition that most of the women in her family are subject to, though she doesn't like to discuss her family with strangers. There's also something in Ellen's way of parsing other people's bodies that reminds her of her university classes in textual analysis. Everything's supposed to mean something else, everything's supposed to be rising, tearing itself free of its wrappings, climbing up to some higher meaning; it's supposed to get away from where it's been. Reality will not suffice. Ellen cannot hide this yearning, and to judge by the many angels she's placed around the room, she doesn't want to either. There are small angelic figures on the desk and in the window, even on a chain around her neck, and now she's on the way over to the other side of the table. She wants to start in on Sonja's feet, which have a defective arch. "They don't want to grab the earth," Ellen has said. It said "Massage Therapist" on Ellen's website, and Sonja thought it would be a form of physiotherapy, but at Ellen's, her shoulder is not a shoulder; it's a feeling. Sonja's hands aren't hands, but expressions of spiritual states. As a massage therapist, Ellen sees it as her job to decode Sonja, and Sonja's only countermove is to decode Ellen. It's a circus of mutual interpretation. If Sonja's wrists are hurting, Ellen says, "Perhaps you're holding the reins too hard." When Sonja says it might also be because the Gösta Svensson novel has her hands toiling at the keyboard, Ellen says, "Then it must be some resistance to Gösta Svensson that's sitting in your hands."

That's not at all out of the question, but now it isn't her hands that Ellen's working on but Sonja's feet, which stick out well past the end of the massage table. Kate's husband Frank calls her "the Masai," because he had once been to Africa. He was down there to tell the Africans about wind turbines, and Sonja imagines him standing in the middle of the savannah. He stands there gazing at a Masai's kneecaps. He's small and clad in a T-shirt next to a man who towers over his head, so now he thinks it's funny to tease Sonja about being a Masai because she's so tall. She's so tall that Ellen's had to scoot her little stool back a few inches in order to really get at her feet. Ellen's good at massage, there's no doubt about that. But with the body analysis, Sonja's gotten more than she bargained for.

"That's a nice pendant by the way," Sonja says, glancing at the angel on the chain.

Ellen fumbles with the pendant and says she bought it at a seminar.

She doesn't say any more, but Sonja's known for a long time that there are some things that Ellen doesn't like to talk about, some additional data. She's partial to the supernatural, and Sonja's friend Molly is partial to that sort of thing too. For as far back as Sonja can recall, Molly's been governed by a geographic and cosmic restlessness. Throughout their years in high school, they laid plans about how they would get away. And it wasn't that Sonja wasn't game. It was more that Molly was the one expanding on the idea, putting it into words. It had been a time of fevered dreams of the future, and that's how they found themselves in a moving van that day in 1992. Dad behind the wheel with his lower lip jutting out, Sonja and Molly with an insistent eastward orientation. First the shared flat, then life in Copenhagen, and then, years later, Sonja found herself at a party at Molly's up in Hørsholm, north of the city. And there there was a fortune teller. Sonja stood and drank a beer up against the fridge while the fortune teller, wearing a curry-colored tunic and drinking just water, was able to see things in Sonja's future. Even though Dad had always advised Sonja to steer clear of anything that reeked of belief, she stood there thinking mostly about how the woman must have some illness, and Dad had also taught her that it was a sin to turn away the sick. So she allowed the fortune teller to let rip. And in hindsight, the fortune teller had certainly been right that she'd be unhappy in love. First she met Paul. Then she fell in love. Then he chose a twenty-something girl who still wore French braids, and the rest of the fortune she repressed. How are you supposed to survive otherwise? she wonders, trying to remember the whole thing. But her memory won't yield.

"Does this hurt?" asks Ellen.

Yes, it hurts, but she doesn't say that to Ellen, because Sonja doesn't want the soles of her feet interpreted, and once in Jutland she also met someone who could see ghosts. She'd applied for a translation residency, because sitting at home with Gösta Svensson had gotten too lonesome. The translation center lay in an old convent, and before long there was rustling under the eaves. There was creaking in the floorboards and doors opening when no one was there. At night, the owls took flight over the main building, and from signs such as these the translators—there were a number of them there—concocted a ghost. The evenings passed with wine and chatter, and in their conversation the ghost walked again. To join in, Sonja gave the ghost some of Gösta Svensson's attributes—the hipster goatee, the tweed jacket, the squeaky shoes. It was easy enough, as she'd translated all his crime novels into Danish and met him several times. What happened then was that she ran into one of the staff members, a chambermaid. Sonja ran into her in the staircase tower; Sonja was going down and the maid was on her way up. "Oh," Sonja said when the woman suddenly appeared, "I thought you were the ghost."

She'd said it to be funny, but the maid didn't laugh. She told Sonja that she could see ghosts. She put her hand up to her left eye; Sonja remembers that clearly, how she fluttered her fingers before her left eye. She said, "I can see the ghosts with this eye." She stood that way, her oddness underscored by the gesture. She didn't seem to want to let Sonja pass; there was so much she wanted to tell her. Among other things, she claimed that the convent was situated in an area endowed with extraordinary energies. Over the centuries, cosmic forces had been pelting down upon the landscape there. In the hills to the west of the convent, there was a place that served as a sacred telephone. She went into a lot of detail, the chambermaid, also mentioning that Copenhagen was the spiritual cesspool of Denmark. The nation's dark energies all flowed to Copenhagen.

"You know, *I* live in Copenhagen," Sonja said.

"Yes, well," said the chambermaid.

"Have you ever driven through Balling?" Sonja asked.

"No," the maid said.

"According to lots of folks, it too is a lovely Danish cesspool," Sonja said, and then they didn't speak to each other again for the rest of the residency.

Sonja looks at Ellen's left eye, which is ash gray. There's a melancholy line around her mouth, and she's stopped tinting her hair. Her hands are powerful, but she's got something dark in the corners of her eyes, and long ago she revealed that she could see Sonja's aura. She also illustrated, with her hand stretched rigid over Sonja on the table, just how far the aura extended into space. "Your energy field is impaired," Ellen said with a quick up-and-down dip of the hand. "You have to let energy in through the crown of your head," she added, and showed Sonja how to use her hands to form a funnel over her head. The energy was supposed to drip down into Sonja like boiling water through a coffee filter.

"On Sunday, actually"—here Ellen squeezes Sonja's feet extra hard, so they'll understand that she's finished with them—"there's this group of women who are going for a little hike."

Sonja nods.

"We're meeting at Klampenborg Station, and then we're hiking to a clearing in Jægersborg Deer Park, where we'll meditate. On the walk in, the idea is to train our senses. Isn't that something that would appeal to you? Wouldn't you like to join us?"

It's because I said her angel was nice, Sonja thinks, not wanting to join them, though she isn't doing anything Sunday. Which is also what she finds herself saying.

"You can ride with me," Ellen says.

"I could also take the train," Sonja says.

"Oh nonsense, it's just as easy for you to ride with me. I leave at ten."

Sonja sits up on the massage table. She fastens her bra behind her back and looks at the cat, which is sitting in the open chink of the doorway. The cat's flat in the face, old as the hills, and regarding Sonja's feet reproachfully. It has no right to look at them that way: her feet may be twisted, but she has inserts to compensate. Then she pays Ellen, who gives her a receipt and assures her that she can deduct the massage from her taxes.

"You're self-employed, after all. Independent."

Independent?

Sonja's standing upright now and can feel that something in her mouth wants to escape. She stands there and chews on it; it feels dry and sticky and adheres to her gums. Home-baked white bread with brown sugar, that's what it feels like, but whatever it is, it blocks the flow of speech.

3.

SONJA'S COME TO A STANDSTILL in front of her mirror. A short while before, she was on her way through the bedroom, sandal in hand, when she caught a glimpse of herself in the mirror on the inside of her wardrobe. It looked as if Kate were standing in the wardrobe. *That's weird*, she thought. Kate and I have never resembled each other. So she stepped over to the mirror to have a proper look.

Kate's got two sons, and her husband Frank. When they're in Copenhagen, they make a beeline for Tivoli, but otherwise they go around trying to disguise the fact that they're from Jutland. Taking Kate out to eat is a trial. It doesn't take anything for Kate to find the food pretentious, and if Sonja asks whether they shouldn't all do the city together, Kate says she just wants to go to a Georg Jensen store, while Frank would rather head to the planetarium.

But it's been a few years since they visited me, Sonja thinks. *And we don't look like each other anyway.*

She moves a little closer, because there might be something in the eyes. There *is* something in the cheekbones and the mouth, though Kate's not as tall of frame. And she looks nicer, more feminine. Back when they were kids, Kate made a big deal out of being the eldest. At the same time, she also was indulgent with Sonja, since Kate was one of those girls who bloomed early. She was so approachable. Mom always said so, before stroking Sonja on the cheek so she wouldn't feel bad about being complicated. Her complications would amount to something, her mother wanted her to know, if she'd simply put her shoulder to the wheel.

Kate's still simple and approachable, puttering around her front yard. She's simple in the neurotic way, but at least she's simple, and Sonja would also be simple that way if only, like Kate, she were able to chase the demons from her body. But because Sonja hides her feelings inside herself—instead of, like Kate, behind the garage, on the sun porch, and under the eaves—she goes to Ellen's for massage. Ellen will lay her warm hands on Sonja, loosen the knots, and get her to notice that her body's there, alive, touchable. It's the sort of thing that others would have a boyfriend for, the sort of thing that men visit prostitutes for; Sonja's just chosen a masseuse in Valby. One with warm hands and a certain predilection for surrogate worlds. That's how she interprets Ellen, since Ellen interprets her, and she feels vulnerable being in a relationship where whatever she is is always supposed to mean something else. And yet she keeps going back. *It's wonderful being delved into*, Sonja thinks, and Kate can't even manage a proper hug anymore. It's become such a boneless embrace, at most the brush of a damp cheek. It's as if Kate can tell that there's something wrong with Sonja; those evasive glances. Now and then they exchange texts, but there isn't really any content in Kate's. Smileys, mostly, and if Sonja calls the landline, it's Frank who answers. If she decides to call Kate's cell, her sister's always standing in the middle of the supermarket, dramatically tapping her foot. She doesn't have time. She's headed somewhere. She's squeezing the avocados, checking expiration dates, flagging down a clerk. It's as if Kate's afraid of something in Sonja, though Sonja doesn't think of herself as a person to fear. *And if there's someone who scares me, it's Gösta,* Sonja thinks, regarding the manuscript on the desk. *His rapes and his sales numbers scare me.* Yet Kate's not afraid of Gösta. That sex criminal who might lurk behind the front door when she comes back from a late shift at the nursing home? Kate tackles him lustily in the pages of Gösta's books. If there's one place the two sisters can meet, it's in Gösta Svensson, because Sonja's in fact the reason that Kate can now disappear, in Danish, into an ordered universe of evil. With Gösta, Kate can sniff death without it actually concerning her, and the hatred she must feel for herself can find an outlet in the killings that always form the prologue of Gosta's stories. She's also told their mother that she feels proud that Sonja knows Gösta. "Kate *is* fond of you," Mom's told her on the phone. "She thinks it's great about that crime writer fellow."

Yet Sonja seldom speaks on the phone with Kate herself.

She tears herself away from the mirror. It's Sunday, and it's time to leave. She wishes she could find some emergency excuse, but what else is she going to do when it's so hot? There will be trees in the deer park, trees and ordinary folks having fun, and so Sonja walks out into the still heat with a water bottle in her backpack.

Ellen lives in a residential neighborhood in Valby. It's not that far from where Sonja lives, and she can see that the people there have means. One day they're building tree forts for their kids, the next, architect-designed sun porches for themselves. Without Paul the Ex—i.e. a man—or a lottery win, Sonja will never end up living in such a place. It may be sour grapes, she knows, but the area makes her queasy: the outsized carports, the extensions, the way otherwise decent single-family houses have sprouted extra rooms and grown into middle-class mansions. Sonja notes with a touch of relief that Ellen doesn't have a carport. She's parked out on the street, waiting.

Ellen's car is silver, and she's wearing hiking clothes and shoes.

"So great that you wanted to join us."

Car interiors often smell a bit stale, but not Ellen's. And it looks like it's been vacuumed.

"Is this new?" asks Sonja.

"Depends how you define *new.*"

Sonja glances quickly in the back to size it up. There's a blanket and pillow, and then Ellen pulls out from the curb without checking her blind spot. They're underway, and it's muggy out. Ellen says that the weather made it hard to pick what to wear. It's mild in that way that might mean rain, and there's a crucifix dangling from the rearview mirror. It's studded with imitation jewels and swings rather frenetically compared to the motion of the automobile.

"How long have you had a driver's license?" Sonja asks.

"Oh, since I was about thirty," Ellen replies.

"Did you find it easy to get?"

"Well, it wasn't that hard."

The car picks up speed and they head down a combination exit and entrance ramp, and in theory Folke had said that they're the most dangerous, so Sonja keeps still. She observes Ellen's feet down by the pedals, her diligent hands, and there's nothing to be afraid of. Ellen has a practical bent, Sonja reminds herself; she's the type that has a grasp of the tangible. She also thinks I should form my hands like a funnel over my head so the universe can dribble energy into me, which means she's got a grasp of the intangible too.

"I think it's hard learning to drive. But you know that," says Sonja. "For instance, I can't shift gears."

Ellen's obligated to maintain confidentiality, and Sonja feels naked and nervous. In actuality, Ellen's not supposed to say anything outside the clinic about what she's heard inside, and now they sit here and have to establish the bounds between professional intimacy and what people ordinarily talk about. Ellen's sworn an oath of confidentiality, something that someone like Jytte could learn a thing or two from, but the borders are ill defined. Sonja doesn't know what to say. She takes the water bottle from her bag while Ellen makes small talk and passes eighteen-wheelers. It's not easy being a patient in your private relationships. Sonja's never liked being someone who has to be taken in hand and assisted. In fact, she's always shied away from others demanding she adapt. Kate was especially meddlesome when they were younger. "Quit your whining," she'd say as she plucked Sonja's eyebrows, for brows ought to sit high, near the hairline, and the hair in front ought to be permed, and shoes and trousers ought to match the rest of the class's, and then here would come Sonja in her yellow clogs. Or worse yet: she and her yellow clogs would disappear into places they should not be. "She's been sitting out in the rye again, Dad," Kate would say, hauling her tall sister into the kitchen. Then Sonja would get an earful, because one shouldn't in God's good name be sitting out in the rye. The rye isn't a playground, it's there to be harvested, and it could be perilous as well if she fell asleep and the combine were to suddenly come upon her. "But I really don't sleep out there," she'd protest. "What do you do, then?" Kate would ask.

Sonja was never able to explain. Not to Dad, not to Kate, and she's always had a feeling that that was what reduced her to an oddball.

Sonja sucks on her bottle, Ellen jabbers away, and the freeway rushes off behind them. Darkness is gathering in the south and it looks like thunder. "Thunder in the south, bring in the cow," Dad would say, and he was right. Sonja doesn't get the logic behind it, but of course it's something meteorological. These days, what she knows most about is how to cast bodies in ditches. Bodies thrown in ditches, the deep woods, lime pits, landfills. Mutilated women and children lying and rotting everywhere on Scandinavian public land. Now and then Sonja takes the train over Øresund strait to traipse around in Sweden, but she's never stumbled across a corpse over there. It's curious, when you think about how many people die a violent death in Ystad alone.

"You read crime novels too?" asks Sonja during a nervous pause.

Ellen does, she must confess. She loves a good crime story. She's read all the novels by Stieg Larsson, and she's also read one by Gösta Svensson.

"Now, I do prefer Stieg Larsson," she says, but that must only be because, during her last massage, Sonja blamed

Gösta for wrecking her wrists. For naturally, Ellen must be wild about Gösta. A big reason for Gösta's success is his tight grip on women. The tweed jacket and the way he's always photographed in the rain.

Sonja's jaw tenses. It's especially the right side, which is having a hard time relaxing. Ellen's also talking too much, and it's mostly about what she had for dinner yesterday and which greengrocers in Valby to steer clear of. She also says that the wrong-way drivers you sometimes hear about on the freeway are in fact suicides. They're just like the people who ram into viaducts and concrete pillars without wearing seatbelts. Wrong-way drivers belong to the tribe who don't want to take responsibility, who don't want anyone to think they did it on purpose. That's the way they think, and Sonja massages the hinge of her jaw a bit. It usually helps with a little water and a menthol drop, but she doesn't have any more of the latter, so she makes do with sloshing some water around her mouth. It eases the ache, and the trip's been a quick one because before she knows it, Ellen's turning into the parking lot by Klampenborg Station.

"Well, here we are, then," Ellen says, and she gets out and stands on the pavement. "The others are waiting by the café."

Ellen doesn't need to point; Sonja knows Klampenborg Station well. She has a secret affection for Bakken, the old amusement park that lies adjacent to the deer park. There's a bakery there where you can eat big wedges of cake at a very reasonable price. It reeks a bit of urine from the bathrooms in the back, but that's all right, because Bakken has a homey air. It's not something that Sonja would be able to explain to Ellen, who was born in Vesterbro before it got hip, and whose parents, grandparents, and great-grandparents were all born well within Copenhagen's tangle of streets and buildings.

Ellen's the one who came up with the idea of meditative hikes. She and a girlfriend figured out the choreography and agreed to activate their network. *Now she looks like she's heading into an oral exam*, thinks Sonja, who has an urge to take Ellen's hand and stroke it a couple of times. And to tell her to not be scared, of suicidal drivers or other women, but they settle for cutting across the parking lot together, backpacks swinging, and besides, who is Sonja to advise anyone? She's got butterflies herself. And restless legs, poised for flight. She also feels a little like crying. Ellen's insecurity is making everything wobble. A person who has her hand on the back of your heart shouldn't be unsure.

4.

AFTER SONJA HAD LIVED in Copenhagen for a year, she discovered something. During a weekend trip back to Balling, she borrowed her mother's bike. She wanted to go out to where the red deer were, the sky, the horizon. Out into the farthest part. But when she got there, the landscape felt empty. It was as if she were standing naked in a swim hall with the pool drained—an echo chamber, and not just any old echo chamber. It dawned on her that it must be her brain playing tricks on her, since back when she'd moved to Copenhagen, the city was overpowering. The sounds, the faces, the odors all seemed chaotic, and she remembered how she'd lain in bed with earplugs and a blindfold. Molly lay in the next room and blossomed, but Sonja had to switch off. She turned down that knob in her brain that let her take in the world at full blast, and once the knob had been turned almost all the way down, the heath, the tree plantation, and the sky overhead seemed empty of content. So she had biked home to her mother with her loss, and a hope: that a knob she could turn down was a knob she could also turn up again.

Could she?

Can she?

Now they stand here, Sonja and the other women. They stand and wait by the café at Klampenborg Station. Each one of them wears light summer clothing and sensible shoes. Somewhere behind them, the sky has started to close up. Sonja glances at the tall trees stretching across a large expanse of north Zealandic countryside. Lightning rods, as far as the eye can see. Dry grass, too many people, and no public taps. Sonja drains her water bottle. Someplace in the distance, she can hear the loud shrieks of someone being swept high in the air.

"And here we have Sonja, who's new."

Ellen's decidedly nervous, and Sonja doesn't like it.

"We'll go up to the deer park first," Ellen says, "and I'll give you instructions once we're up there. Anita will be helping me today."

A small blond woman with round cheeks raises her hand. She's placed herself behind the flock, ready to drive them forward.

"Let's go!"

And so they do. They walk chattering and laughing from the station to where the deer park starts. Ellen waves them in and out among the horse droppings, and after a couple of hundred yards she guides them onto a small path. There they halt.

"What we're going to do now is hike in silence," Ellen begins. "Anita will walk behind you, so you don't get lost in the back. While we're walking, we're going to open our senses to nature. Touch the moss. Pluck the grass, smell the bark, and so on. I think you should also try to make yourself heavy in the pelvis. Shift all your body weight down into your pelvis and let it bear you. It should be as if you're seated within yourself and walking at the same time."

The women seat themselves in their pelvises and move their arms in big circles that Ellen sketches in the air. The women's arms swoop and caper and look like the necks of whooper swans when Sonja would sit out in the farthest part. They'd raise their beaks, the swans, and the organ pipes in their throats would sound so mournful. Not like the call of the bittern, which was more like when the wind sang in the green bottles Sonja had hung in the bird cherry. That sound was as if it came from an unknown place beneath the bird, beneath Sonja, while the whooper swans lifted the landscape up. *Oh, those long necks*, Sonja thinks, rotating her wrists, which is as much as she can manage. She'd weep a little if she were alone, but she isn't, of course. She's captive in the situation, and now Ellen shakes out her arms to indicate the exercise is over.

"Anita and I have been out to reconnoiter," she says. "We've found a suitable clearing, deeper in the park. When we get there, I'll guide you through a meditation. I hope you've brought something for your behinds?"

The women point at their backpacks.

"Questions?"

There are several things Sonja would like to know, but first she needs to get a grip on herself, and then they start walking. The women all walk into the deer park. Ellen foremost, Anita at the rear, and between them seven women plus Sonja. She tries to draw a bit to the side, but it's hard to be part of a group without appearing to be part of a group. And the women are off to a strong start. The first ones have bent over to gather twigs. A short-haired woman has peeled some bark from a tree and is sniffing it. The women begin to inspire each other. The ways one can experience nature through the senses spread. They've walked two hundred yards and the earth has been scratched, fingers have been sniffed, bush and berry squeezed.

Even Sonja's found a cushion of moss. She walks around with cushion in hand so that it looks as if she's taking part. The moss feels wet underneath, she can feel the dampness on her palm, and she sniffs the cushion too; *it smells of sex*, she thinks. Yes, it smells of composting toilets, school camps, secret forts. It smells of the upholstery in scrapped automobiles, the sour tops of fruit juice bottles, and children in grungy undies. She recalls how the old gravel road led in among the firs. Moss grew in the middle, while in the wheel ruts, the stones floundered round in the sand. It wasn't easy to walk in the ruts without losing your footing. But you could walk in the middle, among the dry stalks and tufts of heather—that she remembers. So that's where you walked, and perhaps it was winter, say. First through the tree plantation, then out onto the large section where the sky took hold. Overhead, the universe opened up, and she was traipsing through the landscape in her yellow clogs. Dad had bought them for her at the clog maker in Balling. Actually, she would have rather had some red clogs, but everyone else had bought red ones, so the clog maker only had yellow ones left. At the clog maker in Balling, kids got toffees stuck between their fingers. "Put your hand on the counter," the clog maker would say, and then you were supposed to spread your fingers. The clog maker would stuff toffees between your fingers, toffees that he'd bought cheap down in Germany. The webs of your fingers tensed taut and white. Toffees green, yellow, red, jammed there between your fingers; but there were different kinds of grown-ups. And different kinds of kids. Sonja, for instance, would often sit on a tussock out in the middle of nowhere. Or else she'd sit out in the rye. There was something out there. Something she can't explain to a living soul in Copenhagen, and she can't explain it to Kate either. For Kate, Balling isn't a reason to disappear but a good argument to never leave, and out in the farthest part there were whooper swans. In the winter they'd gather to sing. They might fly out across the plantation but they always came back, and when they came back, the birds that had stayed there on the ground sang to them, and Sonja made her mouth into an O because she wanted to sing along too.

But now she's a grown-up, and it is memory that opens for her. For the landscape won't.

Sonja casts aside the cushion of moss; she has to pee. The bottle of water from the car has run right through her, and she lets herself sift back through the flock. Normally, she'd prefer to squat behind a trunk, a bush. But Anita doesn't know, does she, if Sonja's the type who can only pee in a toilet. Sonja signals that she needs to relieve herself and Anita points into the nearest thicket. Sonja shakes her head; she cannot pee outdoors.

"Just try," Anita whispers.

"It's no use," Sonja whispers back, and she suggests running up to Bakken instead.

Anita says they really can't wait for her. Sonja says that's not a problem, she can just catch up with them.

"But we've found a secret clearing."

"I know the deer park like the back of my hand."

Anita's at a loss, but Sonja can't wait.

"I've really got to go!" she whispers, and feints around Anita.

Sonja runs then, runs in the direction of Bakken. She's got long limbs; her legs are thin, her arms ditto. She's just shy of five eleven. Her hair's cut short, her breasts are small, her eyes big and blue. "You're such a fighter," her mother always said, as if it were some comfort. And it is, for Sonja can keep up the pace, and she keeps it up now. She keeps it up all the way into Bakken. There's actually a toilet by the entrance, but Sonja continues right on into the amusement park. The smell of popcorn descends upon her. Soft ice cream hangs sticky in the air, and she sets her course for The Blue Coffeepot, running a gauntlet of happy Sunday visitors. Tattoos are being aired on shoulders, ankles, and patches of lower back. There are balloons, burgers and papier-mâché façades. The visitors catapult into the air, shrieking, the sky squeaks and squeals. It's one big popular cliché. "A horrible hodgepodge," Molly calls it. "The only reason to go to Bakken is to laugh at the riffraff," she says, since now she's raised herself so far above the losers that she lives in Hørsholm, but it isn't true; Sonja doesn't go to Bakken to distance herself from anyone. She goes there to feel at home, and now she enters the bakery with the giant blue coffeepot and leans over the counter.

"I'm going to order, but first I have to use the restroom—if that's okay?"

It is, and Sonja walks over to the rear of the eating area. She ducks under festoons of plastic beech leaves and steps into the laminated restroom. Here she finds a cubicle with a working lock. They had similar ones at Central Grammar in Balling, where she often went to the girls' bathroom with Marie. There they would sit, each in her own stall, and pee. Sometimes Sonja would try to be funny, and she would sing, "There burbles a spring, there babbles a brook," until Marie giggled over on her side of the divider. Once, when they were all supposed to see the nurse, Marie had forgotten to bring her urine sample from home. She was given a used foil container that had held liver pâté and told to pee in it. Sonja went with her out to the restroom. She distinctly remembers how Marie grimaced with the foil container between her legs. Marie was mortified that her mother had forgotten she was supposed to bring pee from home.

There was usually no shortage of pee in Balling, Sonja recalls as she sits there in the stall. There was pee on the fields, in the kids' beds, behind the clubhouse and in the shrubbery behind the picnic area. And whenever a dog peed on the floor, the owner went over and made sure to rub its nose in it. That's what you did. *It was a kind of pedagogy*, thinks Sonja, and there was probably something to learn from it. She certainly learned something, she thinks as she wipes herself and remembers the women out in the deer park. Their bodies are rocking from side to side on the gravel paths, but Sonja's escaped. Ellen's finding a clearing away from the crowds—Sonja's not there—and now they sit cross-legged, yes, Ellen's sitting there perched on a piece of fleece; the gray hair at her temples damp with sweat, her eyes probing. She's explained to the others that they're to breathe with their abdomens. They're all to close their eyes and focus on their breathing. Silence does them good. Conscious presence opens the now. Yet it's difficult to be present in the now. There's always something tugging you away. A spot itches, or you're afraid of ticks. Or the red deer. The stags will soon come into rut. Then they'll stalk around by the Hermitage Palace and bellow and stink. They'll roll in wallows and prowl about for hinds to mount. They can be violent—no, not violent, brutal. No, aggressive. No, territorial.

Stags are territorial.

Sonja washes her hands and pushes the door open with her foot. She crosses the bakery. At the display with slices of layer cake, she picks the piece with the most whipped cream. She'll have some coffee too, thanks, and then she seats herself in a corner. She digs out her phone and starts texting: *Hi Ellen. Had to use the bathroom. Couldn't find you guys again—I'm such a bumblehead. I'm taking the train back, it's no problem. Sorry!*

The cake tastes better once she's sent the text. In front of the bakery, people gather with their water bottles, sweating. The sky's taken on a sulfurous sheen, and on the other side of the small alley between the bakery and the carrousel, a kid's lucked out. She's been allowed to take a helicopter ride. The helicopter's small and blue and it plunges, up and down, up and down, up and down.

Deus ex machina, Sonja thinks, and washes down the cake.

5.

A VAST EXCHANGE COMMENCES between the earth and sky. A barrel organ grinds and one-armed bandits prattle away in tongues electronic, but in the background Sonja hears a throb. The sulfur in the sky dissipates and turns purple. The trees behind the rollercoaster glow angrily in the last rays of sun, and then here comes the lightning. It begins with a single bolt farther to the north. Then a couple of strikes out toward Øresund strait. Now and then the lightning bolts lash out sidewise at each other and shoot across the sky. The people squeal and seek shelter under the terrace roofs. They have a hard time not getting in each other's way with their fries, and the bakery quickly fills with people. They sit down at the tables with slices of layer cake and cream-filled medallion cookies. They say, "Sure is muggy," and "Lot of water in that sky."

Nothing's as cozy as thunder joe, Sonja thinks. In Balling, they'd sip the black coffee while they watched from the dormer, and it was especially thrilling at their house since they lived at the highest point in the parish. Dad said they were exposed, yet as a rule it was down at the neighbors' that lightning struck. Marie lived there, and her family was Indre Mission. Indre Mission was some sort of sect, and Dad said she should steer clear of anything that stank of religion. Religions were all about corpses that rose from the grave, he said, and not being able to dance or play cards, and he looked at Kate and Sonja with his lower lip jutting out, so they could see he was worried. One time, Sonja wanted to try going to Sunday school with Marie. At first she wasn't allowed to, but for the sake of neighborhood comity her father yielded at last. Then she and Marie had sat there in the meetinghouse and looked at small shiny pictures of Jesus. Marie's dad was there too, and he never said much when they'd sit in their kitchen and press brown sugar into bread. In the meetinghouse, however, he spoke in a loud voice. When the two girls played with Kate in the gravel pit, Marie would often hang upside down from a tree branch. "We can see your panties!" Kate would giggle, but when Marie hung like that she didn't care if her dress didn't stay where it was supposed to. When she sang in the meetinghouse, on the other hand, she smelled of the disinfected linoleum in Sonja's kitchen. But then Sonja's father got into a boundary dispute with Marie's father. They argued property lines till foam flecked in the corners of their mouths. Suddenly Sonja wasn't allowed to attend Sunday school anymore, and that was okay. In a way it was just fine that Dad put his foot down. Indre Mission wasn't that much fun anyway.

People stream into the bakery. Soon there won't be enough chairs, and people begin to steal glances at Sonja's table. A somewhat tired couple approaches. The wife has short permed hair and gold earrings, while the husband's a bit plump and wearing a T-shirt. The thingy from his cell phone is firmly installed in his ear. It thrusts down toward his mouth like a little limb. He keeps speaking out into the air, and Sonja can't tell if it's his wife or someone on the phone that he's talking to.

"All right if we sit here?" the woman asks. Her voice is raspy, her skin gilded with self-tanner and nicotine.

It's Jytte to a tee, Sonja thinks. She nods to the woman. "I'm actually finished, but this weather's for the ducks."

"You can damn well say that again," says the man out into the air.

Sonja does not react, though the man's now staring at her.

"Are you talking to me?" she asks, pointing to herself.

"Christ yes, I'm talking to you," he says, and plops down. He sounds raspy too, and he reaches for the coffee on his wife's tray.

"We saw it coming when we were driving from Ballerup," the woman says. "I told Verner, I told him there'd be a thunderstorm, but Verner said that they almost always head east, over Sweden."

"'Thunder in the south, bring in the cow.'"

"Come again?" says Verner.

"Where I come from, that's what we say: 'Thunder in the south, bring in the cow.' Meaning thunderstorms move north."

The couple from Ballerup regard Sonja uneasily.

"Awful weather in any case," Sonja says.

Ballerup nods. Then they tell her about the torrential rainstorm of 2011, and how much the insurance covered. It's a convoluted account, and Sonja gazes out at the carrousel in the alleyway. It's deserted but hasn't stopped turning. The children have jumped off, and now the horses prance around riderless in the downpour. The carrousel's a lazy

Susan for anyone who seizes the chance. Sonja wouldn't have anything against taking a ride herself. It's nice to do things on your own, to become conscious of yourself and to thine own self be true.

Sonja looks at the carrousel. She hasn't tried one since she was six, maybe seven. Back then, she spoke Jutlandic without irony. Now she no longer knows *what* language she speaks, noting only how the woman's glance flits around the room. Her eyes won't settle on anything, and Sonja's eyes can't help following hers. So their gazes wander restlessly among the faces in The Blue Coffeepot, while the Ballerup woman talks about how the insurance company tried to cheat them.

"We had Verner's instruments standing in the basement," she says. "They were a total loss, but you did get compensated."

Verner's mouth is full of cake, so he confirms this by nodding, and Sonja asks what sort of instruments were affected.

"The Hammond organ and the drum set," the woman says, using a napkin to wipe around her mouth, and Sonja's been at parties where someone like Verner was sitting in a corner and played a fanfare as the ice cream was brought in. And Sonja's clapped at the ice cream and admired the sparklers stuck into it, and she's sung with Verner's refrains about the time the chicken coop was on fire and the rooster wouldn't leave. Kate waited tables at the parish hall for a period, and she probably still does when they need an extra hand. But back then, when Verner played for the entrance of the ice cream, Kate stood there in her starched white shirt, smiling shyly while her face lit up from below. So lovely she was, Kate.

Bakken rumbles and booms, the bakery engulfed in water.

"I think I'll make a dash for it after all," Sonja says. "I'm actually here with a group. They're deep in the woods, and it's not really safe, so I'm just thinking—"

"Yep, you can sure say that again," the man says, and then someone apparently calls him up.

"Yes? Hey there!"

It can't be safe having a phone so close to your brain during a thunderstorm. The father of a boy in Kate's class was once talking on the phone during a storm. That was before telephone lines had been buried in the ground, and lightning struck one of the lines. An inconceivably huge number of volts shot through the handset and into the boy's father, who keeled over on the spot. They resuscitated him before the ambulance came, but still. Kate went out with the boy for a couple of weeks in ninth grade. Sonja thinks she can remember him sitting with Kate in the corner sofa at home, Kate in a pink blouse (so lovely she was), but now the lines have all been buried, if there are even any of them left.

All things pass, and every time Sonja reads something about where she grew up, it's falling to pieces. That way of life is history. Copenhagen's getting bigger and bigger, the papers say. A lowlife property speculator outlines the situation on TV. The kobold on a sinking ship, a shuttered slaughterhouse. Journalists paint a degrading portrait, and the parks of Copenhagen swarm with baby buggies. They're dragged around by flocks of mothers with homesick eyes and dogs on leashes. *Someone ought to start a resistance*, thinks Sonja. Shaming the provinces is just a covert form of deportation, isn't it.

Sonja's made her way to the door, but it's difficult to get out because of all the sodden people who want to come in.

Outside, she joins a knot of visitors under the terrace roof. The alley down to Bakkens Hvile has turned into a creek. A woman in a pair of sopping-wet espadrilles wobbles on the cobblestones. Unattended children have shucked off their shoes and are wading in the water, and Sonja would join them if she weren't a grown-up. Or Sonja would join them if her feet weren't defective. "Your feet don't want to grab the earth," Ellen always says, but now Sonja's bending over. She takes off her shoes and stuffs them in her backpack. She wriggles her toes on the wet cobblestones. They're not unhappy feet. They're not feet that durst not. They *can so*, Sonja knows, and her feet grab hold of the earth. They get a good grip, and then she walks out in Bakken in bare feet. The rain is sluicing down from above and the sewers have thrown in the towel. Yet Sonja walks. She finds it delightful, almost daring, to go barefoot. She walks past carnival wheels and stuffed-animal booths, past shooting gallery tents and vitrines of giant candy. Wasps stick fast to the candy, and the girl who's supposed to be selling it has concealed herself in a poncho. Only her eyes are visible, and they look away. Behind the girl, directly behind her, are the bumper cars.

If I were Frank, Sonja thinks, *I wouldn't hold back. But I'm a woman past forty. Alone in Bakken. Barefoot, and besides, I can't shift gears.*

Sonja stares at the bumper cars. They're driving chaotically around the covered track. All the cars are full, the fathers happy and the mothers where it's dry, clasping prizes.

No, she thinks. *I can't shift for myself.*

6.

SONJA'S SITTING IN FOLKE'S OFFICE. It took a long time to get here, as she kept taking detours. She's been through Frederiksberg Gardens, and she walked down Gammel Kongevej and then back again before taking the side street where Folke's Driving School is located. It's five now; she wanted to catch Folke in the narrow window between when Jytte goes home and when students show up for theory. She'd been standing in line outside the office for a while. There's almost always someone in there with Folke. The youngsters inevitably forget their money and signatures, and the suspended drivers prefer to bring their shame at odd hours, so she feels like a camel looking for a needle's eye to slip through. But now Sonja's seated on the chair across from him. She's asked if they might speak in confidence, and Folke's closed the door.

"I can't change gears," Sonja says, even though that wasn't what she wanted to start by saying.

"I see," says Folke. "What exactly's giving you problems?"

"Everything. Or rather, it's mostly just Jytte."

"Jytte?"

"Yeah, I'm sure she's a good teacher for the younger students. But for an old person like me, I don't think she's a very good fit."

Folke's leaning over his desk. He's a tall man with a bald pate and a striking beard. His face is alive, open, and he's made a concerted effort with the beard. From his chin it tapers to a point, but elsewhere it's thick and bushy. It's as if the hair he once had atop his head has slid down under his chin, where it now points toward his other male hair. He extends his legs under the desk. They're long, and his driving-instructor gut bulges out beneath his hooded sweatshirt. Folke resembles a fat stork when erect and a happy pagan Viking when seated. Or else he looks just like himself, and Sonja likes that.

"What's wrong with Jytte? Is it her big trap, or what?"

"It's more that she loses her temper. She won't let me shift gears, and how am I supposed to learn, then? I get so exhausted when I'm out driving with Jytte that I have to go home and lie down on the couch. And the lessons do cost money."

"Jytte's got a mouth like a longshoreman and a heart of gold," Folke says, leaning back. "You shouldn't take her so seriously."

"But then there was the brawl."

"Brawl?"

It's now or never. So out comes the story of the cross-cultural encounter in the intersection by Western Cemetery. Sonja remembers to include the detail about how Jytte used the horn. The fear, the adrenaline, the hotheaded outburst; the complaints about wrecking Jytte's car. Everything. Folke must be told, and he sits there with his face in worried furrows. He looks like someone who's listening to Sonja, and though she hasn't really thought that far . . .

"I want to drive with you instead."

Folke runs his fingers over his impeccable beard. He explains that he doesn't really drive with that many students anymore. He takes care of theory and administration. He's also hardly at the school when it's convenient for students to drive.

"But I translate Swedish crime novels," says Sonja.

"I don't get it."

"What I mean is that I'm my own boss, in a sense. So I can drive whenever it suits you."

Folke doesn't hesitate an instant but smiles and opens a drawer. Inside is his calendar.

"Let's do that, then, and don't you worry about Jytte. I'll call her. Don't get your head in a twist. It's my business, my responsibility. I'm going to teach you how to shift gears."

Sonja's on the verge of tears. It happens unexpectedly; the sob sits in her throat and wants to come out. Folke's hands move efficiently from side to side across the desk, and she longs to grasp one of them. Squeeze it, say "Thank you," from the heart. It doesn't escape Sonja's notice that she gets red in the face, because this sort of thing rarely happens. It almost never happens anymore—that someone wishes Sonja the best. She's used to dealing with everything herself, and she's reasonably good at it too, but that Folke would reach down in his drawer and face the heat—Sonja hadn't expected that. It isn't that she's planning on the emotion to lead to anything. She isn't. The idea behind getting a license isn't at all to find someone to drive for her. On the contrary, and besides, she's heard that Folke's married to a doctor. She doesn't understand how he pulled that off. *But he's married to a doctor, and that's a good sign*, Sonja thinks, and now he's looking up at her and smiling.

"Crime novels, you say? Did you translate the Stieg Larsson books? They're great. Or that guy Gösta Svensson? My wife's nuts about Gösta Svensson."

Sonja opens her mouth. Her skin stops glowing, but she can't manage any more than that. Folke gives her a yellow note with a date and time for her next driving lesson.

"It'll be Thursday, then." He smiles. "And I'll take care of Jytte. You just go home now and rest."

Then he's towering over her, there in the driving instructors' office. He's taller than Sonja, standing before her in his hoodie.

"Come here!" he says, opening his arms.

Sonja disappears into Folke's arms, his arms like a father's pressing her to his chest. She cannot speak, as she's on the cusp of crying. She also feels bashful. And she hasn't answered about Gösta, but now the moment's passed, and Folke's pushed her away again.

"Thursday," he says.

"Thursday," she echoes, and she decides to take a couple of Gösta's books along when they see each other next.

Then he'll be happy, and so will his wife. Then the lines will be clearly drawn. Then no one will get confused out in the car.

It's the embrace; it was a smidge too intimate, yet pleasant at the same time. It caught her napping. Now she doesn't know how to comport herself, and her cheeks are prickling. She feels like a confirmand, and there's a line outside the door waiting to come in. A long line of youngsters with course papers and passports. Folke lets the door stand open and asks them to move closer, closer. Sonja floats through the theory classroom, painted royal blue. She can smell Jytte in the furnishings, and it won't be long before Jytte knows that Sonja's ditched her for the boss. It won't sound pretty. Then she'll let Sonja have it with both barrels. Then it'll come out that Sonja was never approved by the medical officer, *and she claims it's something with her ears, but you can bet it's something else.*

Something else?

Sonja steps out onto the front steps and into a cloud of cigarette smoke. The rougher students stand around, grabbing a smoke before class. Jytte does the same when she's there during the day, but right now one of the students is describing a driving lesson. The student demonstrates how she turned the wheel too fast. It's an exaggerated movement, and Sonja has to duck quickly to avoid being struck by her cigarette. And in a flash it's there: the positional vertigo.

It's triggered by the dentist position and by bending over too fast, and Sonja has to grab hold of the banister while she restores her head to its proper position. When she gets her head back into place, the world rights itself. The world's where it should be, but it's been shaken. Sonja takes a couple of steps out onto the sidewalk. She doesn't want any of the smokers to see that anything's wrong, and after all, it's not the dizziness itself that creates a problem for driving. She's able to orient herself just fine, as soon as she gets her head out of the angle that triggers the episode. It's more that, for the next couple of hours, she's a tad out of focus. That's not so great in an automobile, but then again it could be worse. And her grandmother could drive a car; her mother too. The first time that Mom got dizzy, she went to the ear doctor, and he had her lie on the examination table and rolled her head around. That triggered a violent attack. Mom's eyes centrifuged and her hands clawed the air while the doctor held her down. He told her she had to lie there a few minutes and "just let the stones settle down."

That helped for a time, but then of course the dizziness returned. It returned when Mom hammered her head against the car's doorframe on the day Kate and Frank were getting married. This was in the parking lot up by the church, and thank God they'd arrived there good and early. Mom got Dad to drive her home with the excuse that they'd forgotten something. Sonja wasn't aware that anything was up, but that might have been due to the dress Kate had stuffed her into, tubular and lemon yellow. Meanwhile, Mom thought she could take care of the positional vertigo herself. Surely the maneuver the doctor had used on her could be performed at home, she thought. She removed the cloth from the dining room table, then took a running start and leapt up on the table so she'd land on it prone, with her head tilted back slightly. The tricky part was catapulting her body up there just right. If she failed, she'd smash her head on the tabletop. Or worse, she'd continue over the table and onto the floor on the far side. But *if* she succeeded, she'd just have to let her head loll backward over the edge of the table. So she took a running start in her heather-colored dress and lifted herself onto the table, landing perfectly. Dizziness assailed her "but the stones had to settle," she explained as she stood in the church later and watched Kate walk up the aisle toward Frank.

Sonja's advanced a cautious distance down the street. Since she's no longer visible from Folke's Driving School, she sits down on some steps. There was a long period when she thought she'd escaped the vertigo. For a while she even imagined that moving to Copenhagen had made a difference. That the dizziness was something social, almost a tradition, she supposed, that you could break with. But then one day she was standing in the entry of her flat and went to tie her shoelaces. The moment she bent over it hit her—the positional vertigo. She crashed into the doorframe and on out to the kitchen and into the stove, before she finally got herself situated so that the fridge stopped moving.

The disorder, she'd thought, and went to see the ear doctor, who proceeded to sling her around. "It's not dangerous, you know," he said on cue. "It's just some tiny stones inside of you that are breaking free."

And the stones just had to settle into place.

Sonja would like to remain sitting there till the sensation of being knocked off course subsides. What she's done for herself is a good thing, isn't it, even though she'll have to get past Jytte now. Sonja's going to be gasoline on Jytte's flames. The smallest hint of a problem with Sonja, and Jytte will set the medical officer on her. If it were up to Jytte, Sonja would never be allowed to learn to shift. She wouldn't even be allowed to drive. She'd be deprived of her right to . . . yes, to what Sonja doesn't really know, but in any case it involves some sort of right, flickering in the back of her eyes like a faulty fluorescent light, and she pictures Mom in a gym suit. The gym suit is shiny and blue, and Mom's feet move swiftly; she's the star of the team. She can do a kick split and spin like a top. She's so stunning that Dad can't take his eyes off her. No way he'd ever get enough of watching a girl like that. Dad takes a running start, he takes a running start and streaks through the gym, his big hands stretching out before him. He wants to get over to where Mom is, and he does. He comes within reach of the girl in the shining outfit. *She looks like a kingfisher*, he thinks, *and kingfishers are rare.* They screech as they fly through the air like arrow shafts, and Mom screeches too when Dad's red hands grasp her about the waist. Then she sinks down; he is gravity itself. "You've got strong arms," she tells him.

And he did, Sonja thinks, lifting herself up off the steps. Strong arms and good sperm quality, and here stands Sonja, in the middle of the great wide world.

She's feeling better, so now she'd like to walk home slowly. She walks down Gammel Kongevej so quietly that she comes to a standstill before the window of a hair salon. Placed in the window are two decapitated heads, a woman's and a man's. They haven't had a change of wigs since the mid-eighties, and the frames of their glasses look creepy. Somewhere behind them, a woman with a silver-tinted perm walks about cutting hair. She's put coffee in front of her customer. The gown's a florid orange, and Sonja can see that the stylist is chatting. Her scissors are busy and so is her tongue. There are two days till Thursday. Two days till Folke's going to teach Sonja to change gears.

Is he going to hug me every time we go out driving? she wonders. *Must I really get more than I bargain for in every single store?*

7.

A TRAIL LEADS INTO THE GRAIN; it's rye. The rye extends high overhead. A few stalks have fallen across the trail, a secret trail that started as a tractor's wheel track. A foot could feel its way forward; and hers did. Afterward, it was a matter of following the rye. You were only supposed to go where it was already bent. If you kept only to those places, you could make a trail so concealed it almost couldn't be seen. In time perhaps, you could bend a few more stalks, make the trail into a path, and then find your way in, deep into the field of rye. The ears of rye have long bristles. The joints sit so high on the stalks that the ears get in your face, and then at the bottom: the sandy soil. The soil's hard, and almost stony, and easy to walk on. One yellow clog after the other. The canteen of juice drink, stuffed into her waistband. And Sonja circles around in the rye like a field mouse. She's made the path herself, and it took her some time. Above her, the sky is endless. The clouds puff upward, the buzzard hangs and quivers. It can hover in the air like a helicopter, and it hangs there with its gaze on the ground. Only its outermost wingtips tremble, and at intervals it straightens its wings. The buzzard hangs like a sketch over Sonja, who's on her way to the hidey-hole. The hidey-hole's a trampled-down lair where the rain's knocked down a patch of vegetation. Even the combine couldn't lift the stalks there, and Sonja seats herself in the hidey-hole. The world beyond disappears, and Sonja sits there cross-legged, like a tailor. She's pushed off the yellow clogs so that she sits in stocking feet. Then she digs out the canteen, and the smell of sweet grain settles around her. She feels like she could actually sing a song right now. A short one, if it weren't that Dad would be able to hear, and she's not supposed to be in the field. The rye's there to harvest, each stalk a part of the crop. The only time kids are permitted in the fields is when they're supposed to find wild oats. "The Devil made wild oats," Dad says, even though he doesn't believe in such things. And the wild oats must be rooted out, or else they'll sow strife with the neighbors. Marie's father in particular has a problem with weed seeds, and kids are the right height, especially when the fields are planted in barley. The bells of the oats dangle above the barley, and Sonja moves like a shark through the surface of grain. Dad walks hunched over behind Sonja, because her sight is good. She can spot wild oats from one end of the barley field to the other, and then she calls out: "Look, Dad, there!" Dad tiptoes like that ballet dancer Sonja's seen on television, in through the grain. Every stalk is money, and it's as if the wild oats might escape. *Snap!* and he's got it, root and all, and he places it carefully in the sack. Then he smiles at Sonja. It's a species of happiness, and once, when they'd come out of the barley, he said, "You're so clever," and Sonja said, "I'm like a little field mouse," and then he placed his warm hand on her head.

That sort of benediction doesn't hang on trees, and now Sonja's sitting in Vesterbro, unable to recall the last time anyone laid a hand on her head. The head's probably the only place on her body that Ellen doesn't concern herself with. Other than now and then massaging points on Sonja's face, but that's not the same. No, it isn't the same, and now Molly's turned up in the chair across from her. The chair rocks a bit, and Molly's busy fitting a piece of cardboard under one of the legs. She's taking a break from her family tonight, she says. The population of Hørsholm will just have to manage things on its own for a couple of hours, for she and Sonja are going to sit in the late August sun and eat well.

Actually, Sonja's not hungry. If she scrutinized herself, she'd find a spot of queasiness. It's not late pregnancy, ha! Or the stomach flu. It's the large quantities of coffee that she ingested during an especially violent chapter of Gösta. All that flesh decomposing; the angry ejaculations, the mutilated vaginas, the ritual adornment of evil. Every summer, journalists ask the members of parliament about the reading material they're bringing to the cottage. And they're bringing Gösta. They don't read anything else, the politicos. In that sense they're like Kate. Both Kate and the politicians brag about the number of crime novels they read. Even though Kate goes around Balling with no idea of improving herself, she imagines that these books are edifying. That's why she tells Mom she's proud that Sonja has a finger in the pie. "Gösta throws light on society from below," people say. "It's just like Sudoku," the politicos say. A crossword puzzle with sperm and maggots, and they're bringing it to the cottage. Sunk in their wicker chairs, they'll read about body parts in black plastic bags. They'll rub themselves in SPF 50 and wallow in evil like it's a party.

I'm a parasite on the colossal cadaver of Western culture, thinks Sonja, feeling queasy. Nausea, sore wrists, and a jaw that tenses as if there's something in there that really wants out, but isn't allowed to exit. Perhaps it's the wreckage of Sonja herself. *Why don't I ever hear from Kate? What's wrong with me? Why the hell can't she just call?*

Then Molly pops up from her mission under the table. Her small heart-shaped face has logged another quarter century of its journey. It's not as though Sonja can't see the high school sophomore in her anymore, for she can. The warmth and the impulses that make up Molly's particular nature still nestle there, glowing deep within like the coals of a slowly dying campfire. It's more that her rules have changed, and Sonja no longer respects them.

They came to a crossroads in their relationship years ago, but no one else in Copenhagen remembers them as they were before that. There's no one else to nourish their roots; only each other. Sonja's one of the few people who knows that Molly's father was a dairyman, while Molly's fully aware that Sonja's the product of agrarian party organizations from western Jutland. In the summer, the girls there played outdoor handball; in the winter they went to gymnastics. There weren't other options unless you wanted to join the Scouts, and Sonja and Molly had more potential. Telling Mom and Dad she wanted to attend the university in Copenhagen was one of the hardest things Sonja's ever done. The light in Mom's eyes, the darkness in Dad's, and after that, Sonja began her language studies and Molly her transformative journey into psychology. She's always been obsessed with escape routes, Molly has. In others, in herself, in Tisvilde Hegn, because for a while she went to an old folk healer up there, a wise woman who was the one who brought the fortune teller to Molly's party. Then Sonja stood up against the fridge and had her fortune told. The fortune teller with the curry-colored tunic and wide eyes, and of course Molly's husband doesn't know, but for a time Sonja was the cover story for an affair with a Belgian who claimed to be a shaman. Molly ran around at his heels up in Hareskoven. They scampered along the narrow paths, squeezing up against tree trunks, folding into and out of each other. He tossed sage around, the Belgian did, and Molly tossed everything else imaginable, for existential dramas create fertile cleavage planes in her mind. At the same time, the lawyer—Molly's husband—has a frank and easy nature that she can hold spellbound, and their kids take care of themselves. It's as if Molly's face has acquired a barred grille, the sort you see in front of jewelry stores. She can yank down the grille in a trice, so that no one can barge in and help themselves to the wares. The technique frightens Sonja.

"I've brought you something," Molly says.

Her chair is standing still now, but Molly on the other hand is rummaging round down in her purse. She finds a small potted plant in there. An aloe vera. It's not quite mature yet, but Sonja ought to have it, and Molly also offers her a cigarette from her bag, though she knows perfectly well that Sonja doesn't want to smoke. Actually, Molly doesn't smoke either, but something needs to happen this evening. *I'm past that age*, Sonja thinks, and she's reminded of the woman at

Bakken with the wet espadrilles. Of course she was drunk. Drunk, and the soles of her shoes as big as bales of straw.

"A fine little plant," Sonja says, rotating the pot.

"It's an offshoot from one of mine," says Molly, smiling, and she tells Sonja about her husband and the kids. They've got so much going on, the kids especially always flying in and out, and once Molly said that her own father had difficulty loving.

He could homogenize the milk in the dairy, pasteurize and prepare it for cheeses that would then ripen into something marvelous, but when he came home, he just stank of buttermilk. He couldn't be bothered with his kids, couldn't be bothered with his wife and hardly even with the dog, but at least he'd drag the dog out for a walk in the neighborhood so it could empty its bladder before bedtime. And the mere fact of that hurt, Molly said—that he was quite willing to take the dog for a walk, but not her. "Because he couldn't love," Molly said, and in Balling there were lots of adults who didn't love their kids. People didn't use the word *love* either. In Balling, you were "fond" of someone if your feelings ran high. But that didn't mean there wasn't any love there. And it didn't mean love *was* there. Kalle's father, for instance, was a socialist, the only socialist in the parish. Everyone else voted for the Liberals or the anti-tax Progress Party, or in a pinch for the Social Democrats, but Kalle's father worked in a factory and was a dyed-in-the-wool socialist. He was also violent. He would beat Kalle, until Kalle stammered so much that he had to take special ed classes. It wasn't as if the teachers at school couldn't see the bruises. Now and then the gym teacher would turn Kalle this way and that in the locker room to examine him. It didn't change a thing: the father was a socialist, a political tendency that invoked brotherly love. Just like Indre Mission and modern psychology. Yet he beat Kalle all the time, until Kalle's speech went to pieces. It wasn't something folks took special notice of; it was worse, they thought, that the father was a socialist. But people did love their kids. Or were fond of them, anyway. No one claimed otherwise, though Sonja knows this much about love: there's not much of it in practice, but it's always thrived on people's tongues.

"It gets rubbed in your face," says Molly.

"Come again?" Sonja's been far away.

"The aloe vera," Molly says, and then she says that someday she'd like to know: where exactly is it that Sonja disappears to?

Sonja places her napkin in her lap, so that it looks as if she intends to take part in the meal.

"I really don't know," she says.

Actually, she'd like to tell Molly that the fortune teller at her party had stripped Sonja of any say over tomorrow, but she's afraid of sharing the story with her. Even though Molly has a master's in psychology, she's drawn to colorful takes on reality. Though Sonja longs for everything the fortune teller might have said to be dismantled, she risks Molly enlarging upon the story if she's given access to it. Clairvoyance! How exciting! It smells of spirits and spooky bedtime stories, and that sort of thing will just stir up the whey that comprises Molly's bedrock experience of life. But Sonja won't have any of it, which is why she hasn't informed Molly of the reading by the fridge. She doesn't even know the fortune teller's name, and for God's sake she'd rather not know. Molly takes a big gulp of wine. The potted plant's a succulent. Or at least it looks like one of those plants that steals moisture from itself, and then suddenly the waiter's there with the food. Right under their noses, potato wedges and burgers. A little bowl of homemade mayo lies sweating on the edge of Sonja's plate. Sonja makes an effort, but she's got no appetite.

"I've been thinking a lot about back home," she says then. "About Kate, for example."

"Isn't Kate well?"

"Yeah—at least I think she is," says Sonja.

Molly raises her wineglass and lets it rest against her cheek. Now she's regarding Sonja as if she were a case study, but Sonja would rather not be a patient in her private relationships; she refuses.

"Remember the day we drove here in the moving van?" Sonja asks.

Molly remembers well. She nods in any case.

"When we were driving across Funen, you said the Great Belt ferry would be 'the point of no return.'"

"Did I say that?" Molly smiles. "I wasn't very good at English back then."

Then she sinks her teeth into a wedge while Sonja looks at the burger on her plate. It's been squeezed between two unruly pieces of bread. The chef has run a wooden skewer through beef and bread to keep them under control, but wouldn't it just be simpler to make the portions smaller? Then Molly leans back.

"Well in a way it was true enough," she says. "And besides, who'd want to go back to Skjern anyhow?"

Molly's face becomes a mask, and Sonja bends over for her bag. Her cell phone. She wants to see what time it is, but then she straightens up too quickly. Her eyes lose focus, and now two Mollies are sitting on the other side of the table—one with a heart-shaped face, the other looking as if she were assembled with caulk.

She closes her eyes, opens them again: still two. She takes a deep breath, because it might have something to do with oxygen. A gulp of cola, and Vesterbrogade buzzes with sunlight. *It is what it is*, thinks Sonja, and she tells Molly that Gösta's going according to plan. She doesn't want to talk to her about back home. That would be like talking to Marie about Indre Mission. That kind of thing's a waste of time, and Gösta's engaged in dissecting the Sweden nobody knows with a fine scalpel, diligently strewing the body parts in a decipherable pattern nearly the entire way from the Arctic Circle to Bornholm. Sonja's a party to the process, she's deep into its linguistic manifestations, and since Gösta's publisher is busy launching Gösta every time he's written something new, Sonja's also busy editing Gösta, so that the blackbirds he's conjured on page ten don't turn into great tits by page fourteen.

"It's also important for a novel that a character have the same name throughout the entire work," Sonja says. "Unless the name change has something to do with the plot, that is."

"Can't you try and translate other authors?" asks Molly. "Some that mean something to you. After all, there ought to be a few Swedish authors who'd like to give readers something besides blood and guts."

"Free market forces," says Sonja and moves her legs; there's really not room for them under the café table.

The aloe wobbles a bit, and Molly proceeds to talk about her clients. Sonja's certain that that's forbidden, but no one's very concerned about oaths of confidentiality anymore. The private has become so trivial and pawed over anyway, and who cares, and so she sits there and watches Molly expound upon someone else's catastrophe. Molly's had a role in the client's life, a life that has gradually turned into chaos. There's hardly anything the client can figure out anymore, so she's started to starve herself. And besides the diet, she's also begun seeing another man, and now her nerves are in tatters—but that's why it's good she has Molly, because Molly has the perspective you're supposed to have at the clinic. She's got the perspective, and a barred grille she can yank down in front of the jewelry shop. The dairyman's deficient ability to love? History. Skjern, and the long, death-bringing canal that was once the Skjern River? Also history. Now the river wriggles like a worm again, out toward Ringkøbing Fjord. One time Sonja biked as far toward the fjord as she could go, and out there lay a stag. Drowned, perhaps, but in any case it was lying on its side in the process of advanced putrefaction. Now the stag has drifted out to sea and the dairyman's dead, but there are still farmers there hunting for one more square foot to raise corn in, and the place you come from is a place you can never return to. It's transmogrified, and you yourself are a stranger.

"How's it going with the driver's license?" asks Molly.

"Bumpily," Sonja replies.

She relates how Folke pulled her close in the driving school office.

"You think I'll have trouble with him in the car?"

"I think you already have trouble with him in the car."

Molly dips a wedge. Then she looks at Sonja and says she could also try her luck. See what Folke has to offer.

"Oh Lord," says Sonja, but the images have already made themselves known:

Sonja and Folke on the backseat of the car. Or in front, her one leg over the headrest, the sole of her other foot on the instrument panel. Arms splayed and folded the best they can, Folke's little ass sticking out the door. The slap of belly on belly, the penetrations, the damp spots on the blanket.

"And what's that supposed to lead to?" Sonja asks, thinking of Paul the Ex, whose ass was relatively compact as well.

"A bit of street action," says Molly.

"He's married to a doctor."

"So?"

Which men belong to which women isn't a topic that interests Molly. Life ought to be kept at a boil, dramas a-simmer, and beneath the love you never had there should be the roar of tinder-dry twigs catching fire.

"It's just not me," Sonja says, and she peers up Vesterbrogade.

A helicopter approaches overhead and follows the street up toward Frederiksberg Boulevard, where it veers off. It's yellow and orange and looks like the kind that flies doctors around sparsely populated areas. But that's not what's best about it. *What's best,* Sonja thinks, *is that it can rise straight up and down between asphalt and sky*, and she starts to hum. Molly's in the midst of her burger and a long explanation of love's paths and detours, but Sonja's sober, and she hums. She hums the one about the little lark. She hums the passage where the bird takes flight. *You take the straight way from Earth to Heaven*, she hums.

8.

Dear Kate,

So now we're writing each other postcards? you must be asking. But it's just that I found this card with heather on it and thought you should have it, since I suppose it must be blooming now, the heath. The other day, I also came to think of how you'd often find me out in the rye. Funny, because I haven't thought of that in years. I'm sure I wasn't easy to keep tabs on, ha-ha! Hope you're doing well. As for me, I'm finding Copenhagen on the muggy side. The driver's license is coming along (another ha-ha!) and so's work. I'll set aside a copy of the new Gösta Svensson for you. Then you can get it when we see each other. Or I could send it—it's up to you. Hello to the family, and I'll talk to you soon.

Hugs, Sonja

Sonja's folded the postcard and stuck it in an envelope. All that's left now is the addressing and stamping, but she's not really sure about that. In truth, she wasn't thinking of sending the card. If she were going to send something that sounded like her, it would sound different, but she's not sure that Kate likes her when she sounds like herself. She decides not to send the postcard. *I should have written it to Mom instead,* she thinks. *Mom loves heather.*

Sonja takes the postcard back out of the envelope. She places the card with its pleasant image of heather in the wastepaper basket beneath the desk. Then she takes out a clean sheet of paper and her favorite black marker for writing with:

Dear Mom,

I was just sitting here thinking of you. I also thought of you the other day, because I was thinking of the rye. I used to just out there in the rye, enjoying myself. Sometimes Kate would drag me out. I don't know if you can remember it, but I remember you standing behind the windbreak and calling me. It was nice that you knew where I was, even if it was a place I wasn't supposed to be. But why wasn't I actually supposed to be there? What was it that Kate and Dad had against it? A couple of stalks, good grief. But in any case: I miss places like that. My apartment doesn't do the trick. Sometimes I lie down over in the cemetery to get a bit of the effect. The other day I nearly sent you a text saying, "Hey Mom, I'm lying in the graveyard." (Ha-ha-ha!) I'm not, not in that way anyhow. And fortunately, you aren't either. Not yet, that is. But what am I going to do when you are? I think about that often. That I'm going to miss having family members who understand me, and it'd be nice if I could get Kate in conversation. I know it makes you sad that we can't seem to get along. I'd like to. I'm also trying to, but never mind that now, because I hope you and Dad are doing well. You guys should stick around for years, of course. Otherwise there's nothing new to report, other than it's not going so hot with the driver's license. I can't change gears. I'm so fond of you, Mom.

Hugs from your Sonja

Sonja regards the letter. Then she crumples it up and throws it in the wastepaper basket. It's lying on top of the postcard now. It's lying there crumpled up with its black letters, on top of the picture of heather. *It's hard to find clothes to fit the body you have, and it's hard to find words to fit the people you love,* Sonja thinks, looking at the aloe plant that Molly brought in her purse. "I take a leaf every morning and cut it into pieces," she said. "Then I rub it around my face. It soothes and moisturizes."

Sonja runs a finger along the aloe's sharp, tongue-like leaves. With her other hand she probes her face where the skin is soft and working its way loose.

She tries to recollect the fortune. She rummages around in her mind for what the woman in the curry tunic said as Sonja had stood there, leaning up against the fridge. What lay in wait for Sonja as a woman? More of the same, or a break? The unhappy infatuation with Paul, naturally, but what else—a tragedy? A catapulting, a happy ending?

She can't recall. She's removed it from her consciousness and placed it in storage. She's afraid that it'll become true if she remembers it, or else she's afraid that it'll lose its power if it's brought to light. She's afraid of not believing and she's afraid of believing, and she remembers how, several years ago, she went into the church back home. She just wanted to sit a bit and talk about the fortune with something bigger. It was nice to let go of things and then gamble that Something Bigger was listening and wouldn't blab to Dad, who feared Something Bigger, because its existence would tear him from the reality he knew. Members of Dad's family shouldn't tear themselves from the reality he knew either and then leave him there alone, but here she was, sitting in Balling Church. First pew, the one up by the baptismal font. On the chancel arch there hung a pale Jesus, and then there was the altarpiece, where the risen savior was depicted with a defective left leg, for the hardest thing to draw is foreshortening. Anyone who's tried to draw a person from below knows that; giants become dwarfs, but there Sonja sat, chatting with Something Bigger about the feeling of not being able to fill her life in the right way. *It was pleasant,* Sonja remembers. There was something reassuring about sitting there and trusting someone besides herself.

It also felt as if someone had answered inside her, telling her she mustn't lose her grip, for there was someone to whom she would one day become a source of pleasure. Someday she would come to someone's rescue, yes. She must believe that. In the end she had said the Lord's Prayer, the way Marie had taught her when they were kids, with a singsong emphasis on the words, and then she went out into the vestry before anyone discovered her sitting inside and being holy. She also had to pee, but then the door was stuck. The door leading from the vestry was jammed. She heaved and hauled on it;

it wouldn't budge. It was as though her fear about roadside churches—that someone would lock her inside—had been realized. Her communion with Something Bigger turned to silent panic. It was nice talking to Jesus and those guys, but she didn't want to be locked up with them. She also had to pee, she really had to pee, and over there was the collection box, there was the font, there her sacrilege, so she heaved and hauled on the handle till she barked the skin off her knuckles, and finally it hit her that she had her phone in her pocket. There was contact info for the church employees tacked to the bulletin board. The sexton's name was Niels Jørgen, and she had a hard time placing him in Balling's topography, but what she did was to ring up Niels Jørgen. She remembers the conversation clearly as she sits and rubs a stub of aloe vera around her face.

"Niels Jørgen," Niels Jørgen said on the phone.

"Sonja Hansen. I'm over in the church and can't get out."

"You can't get out?"

"I'm standing in the vestry, and I can't budge the latch. I've just been in here for a little while, sitting in the church. Did you lock me inside?"

The instant that Sonja asked about it, the door opened. She'd attempted to try the door one last time, just to illustrate to Niels Jørgen that she was trapped in the situation. And then she wasn't trapped in the situation after all.

For a long time after, she felt that whenever she told someone the story, the power would drain out of it. And there *was* power in the story, something significant in it that was hard to put into words. She still feels that way about the fortune. She doesn't believe it, but there's something there that might vanish if she lets light fall upon it, so she keeps it in the dark, down in the dark with her future, and the aloe around her face.

And her and Kate? When did their break start to show on the surface? A few years with separate lives, and then a microscopic crazing in the enamel. She'd noticed the tiny cracks, and no doubt Kate saw them too, but Sonja can barely recall when it became obvious to her. She supposes it was fall. Yes, it was one October, she thinks, and they'd taken a walk around Balling, she and Kate. On the eastern end of the village outskirts lay Østergård. Sonja remembers back when the farm had resembled an ordinary farm, but after Bjarne took it over, the barns sprouted narrow extensions that stuck out on every side. As the two approached the farm, they managed to get through Kate's routine worries, her fear of burglaries, and the pain in her knee.

But then at some point they'd reached Østergård. The farmhouse sat there diminutive and forlorn in a small cityscape of long extensions. From inside the piggeries came the rustle of bodies against metal, and while Kate busily expounded on her workaday fears, Sonja caught sight of the narrow strips of ground left between them. No architect had been consulted on how to best expand the farm, or how the ground plan could be harmonized. The pig barns had been knocked together in no time, and there were all these narrow strips of dead space between the extensions.

"See," Sonja interrupted. "That's negative space there. If the Devil himself had to live someplace, he'd pick one of these appendixes."

Kate stopped and stared into the long dark ravine between a piggery and an equipment shed. At the end of it was a gray cinder-block wall, and out of the earth there poked withered weeds of some indefinite species. The ground reeked of ammonia.

"Don't you see?" Sonja asked. "Only the Devil himself could live in such an intestine. Any life, any form of aesthetics, communication, or love—they've all vanished from in there. It's the ultimate non-landscape."

Kate stared into the constricted patch between piggery and equipment shed. Her eyes wide open in the twilight, a childlike expression on her mouth. Silent.

"Not even chickens could survive in there," Sonja went on. "Not even a couple rows of potatoes," she said. "A dead landscape."

Then Kate had started to walk, quickly. Sonja had to almost run after her, and she wanted to ask what was up. But when she caught up to her, Kate refused to be led or driven. It was all about the pork loin that had to go into the oven, Frank who had to be picked up from soccer, and his sweatsuit wasn't going to wash itself, was it?

Sonja looks at the aloe where the leaf's broken off. Small droplets are oozing from the stump. Essential oils, no doubt, soothing. So she reaches for the pot, which feels nice and warm. *I can use the pot in any case,* she thinks, and she sticks her hand down into the soil and uproots the entire plant. The contents of the pot feel sticky in her hand. The leaves of the succulent poke up from the soil like knives. Or tongues. Or fingers that are reaching for Sonja's face and mouth. *A vulgar plant,* she thinks, throwing it into the wastepaper basket. There it lies, atop the heather, atop the letter, atop the things she cannot find the language to say and the people she most wants to say them to.

9.

BECAUSE FOLKE'S LARGE in every way, he's got a car to match. That's not something Sonja had considered in switching driving instructors; that she should go from Jytte's Hyundai to an Audi Q5. It's the size of a camper, black as a Batmobile, and Folke's sitting in it with beard outthrust.

"Today I want to test you," he says.

"Test me?"

Sonja casts a sidelong glance at the bag of Gösta that she's just deposited on the backseat. The books are for Folke to take home to his wife.

It's also Sonja's plan that they'll talk about Folke's wife as much as they possibly can. It should be as if she's there with them in the car. The wife and Gösta and Folke and Sonja.

"I need to see, of course, what you've learned with Jytte, so now we're going to drive into a neighborhood where the intersections are unmarked."

"You'll help me with the gearstick, won't you?"

Folke points down in between the seats.

"There it is."

"It's not the placement, it's the handling," Sonja says, but she shouldn't have.

Or rather, she shouldn't have said it in quite that way. Now Folke's compelled to quiver his eyebrows. He's compelled to tell her that obviously she's a big girl. Sonja pretends that she doesn't understand the sexual innuendo. She's not paying four hundred crowns an hour for sexual innuendo.

"It's nice that your wife's a reader," she says, putting the car into first gear.

She's able to do that just fine. She's also able to look back at her blind spot. She signals and drives away from the curb; second gear.

"Pretty good," says Folke, and he directs her into a neighborhood with unmarked intersections.

Neighborhoods with unmarked intersections are Sonja's bugaboo. It's not only that nobody knows who's supposed to yield to whom. It's also because people park along the curbs. That makes the streets so pinched, they get scarily narrow and are studded with cars whose doors open suddenly, temperamentally. Sometimes the parked cars function as hiding places for kids, and kids' lives are governed by impulse.

Back when Sonja drove with Jytte, Jytte also kept telling her to "STOP DRIVING INTO OTHER CARS' EARS!" Naturally, Sonja didn't know what that meant at first. But the ears turned out to be their side-view mirrors, and Sonja wasn't supposed to drive into them, and now Folke and Sonja are alone in the car. Sonja pulls herself together in every way. She and Folke both have their seats pushed back so that their long legs have room. Her feet pump the pedals, her fingers clench the wheel. They clench the wheel so tight that she automatically veers left when she lets go with her right hand to change gears. It's difficult to find third. Her driving's unsteady, and Folke's Audi is too big for the street they're going down.

"Work with the car, use your body, use your body!" says Folke.

But Sonja's body cannot get from second to third. She's stalled twice now.

"Then let's pull over here to the side," Folke says in a soft voice.

He helps her to turn the wheel as well. Someplace over in the bottom of Folke's side of the Batmobile he manages to brake, and now they're satisfactorily stopped behind a Toyota.

"Give me your hand," Folke says, and she doesn't want to, but she gives Folke her hand anyway.

He takes the hand and places it on the gearstick.

"Can you feel it?"

She can, and then Folke places his hand over hers. Sonja can now feel both the gearstick and Folke's hand. Then he begins to move their stacked hands: the gearstick is activated.

"You have to imagine an H with two segments poking out of the middle, and then we do like this . . ."

You can*not* make diagonal movements with the stick, Folke explains. You can*not* go from second to third by taking a shortcut. You *have* to follow the construction of the gearbox. That all makes sense to Sonja, but she has a hard time concentrating with Folke's hand on top of hers.

"There," he says, and lifts his hand. "Now we'll try it in real life."

Mirror, shoulder, signal: Sonja tries to use her body, but the car's too big.

"Throw the car, c'mon, throw it!" he exclaims.

But is it even possible to throw a car? Is it possible to do from the inside? Driving instructor lingo makes Sonja insecure, and she's insecure enough as it is—with the car, the gearstick, the social aspect of the situation. Her insecurity's due to an underlying fear of inadequacy, Molly would say. It's awful being a disappointment to both yourself and others, and Sonja's solution is to talk. Speech has horsepower and direction. With speech, she can do what she can't do with the car: she can throw it, and if she just jabbers away, she'll become a person in Folke's eyes.

"I completely forgot to tell you, but it's me who translates Gösta Svensson into Danish," she says.

"Get out of here!"

"The bag on the backseat's for you," she says. "It's got books. You can give them to your wife."

Folke rotates his large body around and grabs hold of the book bag. Back in the front seat, he immediately starts pulling books out of it. Gösta's novel *Black Blood* flies up onto the dashboard. Same for *The Girl from Riga*, "a harrowing read about human trafficking," as one reviewer's quoted as saying on the back cover. Folke's thrilled. He forgets to advise Sonja on her driving. That doesn't matter, because it's going better with the gears, while Folke leafs through the books. He wants to know if translating's hard. He also wants to know if there's any money in that shit, and he wants to know where Sonja learned Swedish. In this way, she gets a chance to tell him that she's the first in her family to go to university. Her sister's a home care assistant, and her brother-in-law works at a wind turbine plant. Sonja also succeeds in saying that her father's a farmer, and that she comes from a parish that lies so far west that Folke's probably never been there.

"Nope, never been that far from Copenhagen. I've been to Croatia, Germany, and large stretches of France. But nothing beyond that. I only go places you can drive to in a car. I'm afraid of flying."

"I love flying," says Sonja.

Folke gives a convincing display of fear on his side of the car, and once Sonja read that men who are unfaithful exhibit an especial fear of flying. They project their fear of being caught in infidelity onto the flying situation. Being unable to escape. Being at the mercy of another man, the pilot. They can walk around and feel reasonably fine about their deceit down on the ground. But at altitude, the consequences dawn on them in a different way. They realize that they don't have solid earth underfoot, that they risk losing it all. Because you really can; you can risk losing everything when you lie.

Sonja winds through a chicane designed to slow traffic. Folke claps her on her gear hand.

"But anyway," Sonja says, getting her hand back up on the wheel, "where I come from, things aren't the same anymore."

"Oh no?"

"No, the farming operations have gotten so huge," she says. "They buy up everything around them. My parents' farm was bought up by a hog breeder they call Bacon Bjarne. Now my folks live in a house in Balling. My sister too. That's why the smaller farms stand empty, and when they're empty, there are no families with kids living there, and when there aren't kids, there's no one to go to school. Then the schools close, and when the schools close the whole thing shuts down. Bacon Bjarne doesn't care two straws—as long as he can make the payments on his outrageous loan from the credit union, it means nothing to him if the infrastructure goes south. My dad always said that people are strange vermin, and he's right. But the deer are still around. There are so many deer that they have to make exclosures for them."

"Exclosures?" asks Folke, indicating with his hand that she's too close to the other cars' ears.

"They're the opposite of enclosures, like they have for cattle."

It's good to talk and drive at the same time.

"It's for keeping the deer out of the crops. They can flatten a field of grain otherwise. You have to imagine two, maybe three hundred animals the size of horses suddenly getting into the grain. They tramp it all down, and once the stalks are bent . . . It's the sort of thing that farmers worry about a lot. So they make exclosures. There are hairdressers there who sell farmers the hair they cut from the locals. Then the farmers put the hair in potato sacks and hang them on fence posts by the exclosures. Because human hair scares off deer. They don't like the smell, and then they go somewhere else, but they're there anyway, the deer. They're in the tree plantations and out on the heath, and sometimes a lone deer will wander off from the herd. Pretty soon they'll be going into rut. Then you can hear them when it starts to get dark."

Folke emits a deep guttural sound from over on the passenger side. It sounds as if he's growling. Yes, Folke's growling, and Sonja swerves around a cyclist.

"Anyway," she says, "I didn't intend on becoming a translator. I wanted to write books—but then again, doesn't everyone?"

"You can't make a living from that sort of thing," says Folke, and he shows her his fingers. They're long.

"Guitar," he says. "But if everybody played heavy metal, then there'd be nobody to teach you to drive, and if you wouldn't mind paying attention to the rules about right of way here . . ."

He directs her into the parking lot of a supermarket in Hvidovre. Around them, peaceful morning shoppers move about. Folke and Sonja drive slowly, slowly, and as they circulate, Sonja gets more and more of a handle on the distance between second and third. Folke holds forth on the right of way at unmarked intersections, and Sonja says that Gösta isn't really that tall. He's a bit bald as well, but he's got a house on Gotland with big picture windows. Gösta can see the ocean. It stretches like a vast plain all the way to the mainland. Sometimes at night, Gösta dreams that he's walking out on the sea. He walks, jogs, and runs, all the way to Oskarshamn, where the real Sweden begins. The Sweden where there are forests and stone quarries, moose hunters. The Sweden where weapons manufacturers lie and simmer beneath it all. That's the Sweden he wants to describe, and Gotland's a good place to do it from.

"Part of how I get paid is complimentary copies," Sonja explains, holding back for a shopping cart on the right. "My storage space is stuffed with crime novels and historical romances and so forth."

Folke says he's sure his wife will be happy to get the bag. She's a foot doctor in Roskilde, and when she's off work, she'd rather not think.

"She's a foot doctor?"

"A top-notch orthopedist," Folke says, smiling, and he flips down his sunglasses.

The car rolls peacefully along with Sonja and Folke while he fiddles with the ventilation controls.

"And Jytte's okay?" asks Sonja.

"Don't you go troubling your head about Jytte."

"Well, but she probably wasn't very happy, was she?"

"That's all behind us now."

Sonja doesn't know that it is. It might well be that Folke's not afraid of Jytte. Sonja doesn't feel so serene, but what he probably would have her understand is that Folke, like the man he is, settles matters as they arise, while women keep them going. And yet Dad still bears a grudge against Marie's father because Marie's father lopped branches off the wild apple on Dad's side of the property line in 1979, while for his part, Marie's father can't forgive Dad because Dad threw foxglove seed over on Marie's father's side of the brick transformer tower. Nowadays when they walk around Balling, they lift their caps when they pass each other, full of ill will, and that's the kind of people Jytte comes from. Jytte and Sonja.

Folke rolls his window down a chink.

"Bacon Bjarne," he says, and laughs.

"He was my sister's boyfriend once."

"Folks are damn funny. We had a fellow we called Stove Hood, down on Sønder Boulevard. But Bacon Bjarne."

"He's not very funny in real life."

"Nah, but who is?" Folke sighs and sticks his hand out the window. "What an August. I tell you the sky was banging the earth like billy-o on Sunday."

Now he laughs again. Sonja does too, a bit, even though Folke shouldn't be saying *bang*. No, he shouldn't say *bang*. But Sonja can hardly control the car, so how's she supposed to control Folke? She looks down at her hand. Then she discovers something, like some objective finding. On its own, the hand has gone from third to fourth. The distance between third and fourth is a straight line from above to below. *A simple distance*, thinks Sonja. *No diagonals.*

10.

Sonja calls up Kate but it's Frank who answers. Nothing new in that, of course, though Kate's normally someone who likes to talk on the phone. As a teenager she hung out on the phone all the time. Mom would get irritated at Kate for all that chattering. "You and then Dad and all your talk," she'd say. "What is it that's so important?"

Mom's world exists within herself. She doesn't need to ring up the world outside. It's only if someone's died or ended up in the hospital that she uncoils the telephone cord. That's a trait that Sonja's inherited from her, but it can also get too quiet, and you ought to call your family once in a while. So sometimes Sonja calls home. It's best if Dad doesn't pick up the phone, because he's spent too much time driving farm equipment. Hearing protection's for big-city farmers and sissies. A whole generation of tough guys is walking around now with batteries behind their ears. They make noise in the theater foyer and the quiet car on trains. They rustle their newspapers and invade conversation. Dad has a hard time hearing what Sonja says on the phone. She has to yell into the receiver. She doesn't have the energy; she retreats. Then Dad stands there in his lonely majesty and shouts across Jutland. It lacks dignity, and Mom really doesn't like to talk on the phone.

But now Sonja's called Kate. She's called even though Kate won't answer the phone. *Perhaps she's gotten caller ID*, thinks Sonja. *Perhaps Kate goes over to the phone and glances at the display: "It's Sonja," she tells Frank. "Can you take it?"*

If Sonja and Kate were apples, you'd say that they'd fallen on two different sides of the tree. It's true. That it also feels as if someone's kicked the Sonja apple so it's vanished deep in the tall grass is another matter. But that's how it is; the Sonja apple lies somewhat repudiated in the grass. Now Kate doesn't know what to say to her anymore, which is why it's good she's got Frank. He can talk to anyone, and he doesn't hang back either. He goes right up to people, and he isn't afraid to get down to the nitty-gritty with Sonja.

"I suppose you're going to start looking at cars pretty soon, right?" he says.

"I just have to get my license first," says Sonja.

"You haven't gotten it yet?"

"I've changed driving instructors."

"It was a woman you were driving with before, wasn't it?"

Sonja cannot deny that Jytte's a woman. Frank makes a sound, and she can tell exactly what the sound's supposed to indicate, but she doesn't rise to the bait.

"Yes, I've changed instructors, so something should happen pretty soon now," says Sonja, even though she's unsure.

For what if nothing happens? What if it's the same thing all over again with Folke? Maybe Sonja's one of those people who *can't* drive. It's not just a question of medical officers and the denial of certain existential rights. It's also a question of spatial talent. She knows this because she once saw a show about a psychology professor. He had the same name as a certain provincial town, and he liked to put women in a centrifuge. He'd had the centrifuge constructed for his experiments. A woman would sit strapped into the middle, and Gösta would have loved the contraption. If Gösta knew it existed, he would immediately write it into a scene. A woman, strapped tight and preferably naked, with something in her mouth. But never mind Gösta, because then the psychology professor centrifuged these women. The women were spun around, up and down. They spun in ellipses, and yes, they were strapped in while they spun. Then afterward, when the centrifuge had stopped, the women were asked to do exercises. In the exercises, they were supposed to orient themselves spatially. They were supposed to coordinate distances and solve math problems and walk a straight chalk line. The women were terrible at it, and the professor concluded that women were poor at orienting themselves in space. Then he put a black man in the centrifuge. He centrifuged the black man for a long time and achieved the same result: black men were extremely bad at orienting themselves in space. In fact there was only one group of people who oriented themselves worse, and that was black women. Black women were decidedly out of it, the psychology professor declared. *White men, by contrast,* he concluded after having given himself a ride on the swing, *are patently the best,* and everyone made the sign of the cross. *Garbage in, garbage out!* people yelled, and Sonja yelled with them, but who was she to get all steamed up? She with her inability to shift, her positional vertigo?

"Have you thought about what kind of car you want to buy?" Frank asks.

Because Frank works in a wind turbine plant, he's the one in the family who knows about technology. He and Kate drive a station wagon themselves, but he thinks that Sonja has money. Everyone who's gone to college has money. On the other hand, Sonja doesn't have a proper job, so she's probably broke. This uncertainty is lodged deep in Frank, and it arises often in their conversations together. One moment, Frank thinks she should buy a villa on the posh side of Copenhagen. The next, he thinks she's better suited to a row house in a small town whose residents are starting to flee. Now she should get a silver Citroën.

"And yet maybe after all," he says, thinking aloud, "you might be better off with a used vehicle."

Sonja thinks about Folke, centrifugal force, and the fact that perhaps she's utterly incapable of learning to drive.

"A lot of them have logged more than 80,000 miles and still drive perfectly fine," says Frank. "If you're able to fix them up a bit yourself."

Sonja's quiet on her end of the line. On Frank's end, the dog's barking.

"Turn down that dog!" he shouts into the room.

So there is *someone home*, thinks Sonja, and at first the noise continues, and then it grows quiet.

"What kind of dog do you guys have these days, actually?" asks Sonja.

"A golden retriever," answers Frank.

"Ah, a real family dog."

"Yeah, Kate really likes golden retrievers," Frank says, though in fact it sounds more like a sigh.

"They always use golden retrievers in movies," says Sonja.

"At one point, I saw so many golden retrievers in Hollywood movies that it got suspicious. Tom Hanks pretty much never appeared without one. But the intriguing thing was that black Americans on screen never had golden retrievers. The golden retriever was a white family dog. The blacks had dogs they could keep in their pockets. Or dogs the size of garages. It was one or the other with black family dogs."

Now she's lost Frank, and she also catches sight of the drawing she's made on the piece of paper next to the phone. It's a doodle. Within the doodle, a distinct shape has appeared. Inside the shape sits a little figure, waving. The figure waves at Sonja from inside its handsome helicopter. *Soon the ladder's going to drop*, Sonja thinks. *Soon they're going to let down the lines and come to my rescue. Then it's up to me to clamber up. Not to be scared. To grab hold and let myself be borne away, through the air and over the heath, the plantations, the inland dunes. Someplace below lies Balling and the next-door parishes. Frank in the backyard with a golden retriever. Kate directing her fear into the cold cuts, the septic tank, the water heater, and then into the kitchen with the hand mixer and fondant. A grocer, a feed store, an apple tree that has cast its apples. A trail that leads into the grain.*

"You could also buy a Jaguar," says Frank. "You can get them cheap in Germany, if you fudge on the plates."

It's strange that he says that, for Frank would never be able to fudge anything. A spot of under-the-table work perhaps, but Frank does things by the book. After all, those wind turbines don't hoist themselves up on their own. Sonja knows that, and now he's telling her how they raise them into the air. How they place them at the base of the tower. It's a balancing act.

"A bit like those Chinese acrobats who spin plates around on sticks," says Frank. "But just try multiplying that by a couple thousand."

Sonja can see it before her: thick columns with immense platters, spinning. The turbine propellers in ellipses, up quick, down quick.

"The turbines actually look a bit like helicopters," Sonja says.

She hasn't thought about it before, but they do. Frank grows quiet on the other end of the line.

Then he says, "Kate's afraid that they're going to fall down while I'm up inside them. Or underneath them. Of course for me, up there's often the nicest place to be. It gives me something to tinker with. But Kate's scared that they'll be defective, or I'll get electrocuted, or whatever it might be this time. You know what it's like, Sonja, it could be almost anything, and then we bought the dog. Having somebody to take care of—it's good for Kate."

It's true. And Kate's good at taking care of somebody. But she won't take the phone when Sonja calls.

"Is she home there with you?" Sonja asks, carefully.

"She's out with the dog," says Frank.

Of course she is, thinks Sonja. *Out with the dog, and I'm out of the picture.* And yet not entirely. For Sonja feels stuck. It's a strange paradox. She feels like an escaped prisoner with big chunks of concrete under her feet. It's hard to walk this way. *It can't be good for my balance*, she thinks, and then it's time for them to hang up, her and Frank.

"Say hi to Kate," says Sonja.

"Done!" says Frank.

So she must be sitting next to him on the couch, Sonja thinks. *Kate must be sitting on the couch, not knowing what to say to me.*

The conversation's over, but it persists in Sonja like a downpour. A feeling of sorrow percolates down through her, seeping in and out of her internal organs, picking up pebble and gravel on its way. She doesn't cry, she can't let it get that far, but within her there seems to be a rattling; from little stones, from stalks, from days where it never quits. Inside her the sky empties itself in slow, unresolving fashion, and there isn't anything worth naming in the fridge. Then she looks out into the backyard. There isn't anything worth naming in the backyard either, except for the owls. The owls are there to keep the pigeons off the balconies, and they're plastic, the owls are, but the pigeons don't know that, and besides: who told the neighbors that owls are prophylactic? After all, the neighbors have fled nature to sit and drink beer on their balconies. They've all got a plastic owl on the balustrade, and the owls are supposed to frighten, intimidate. She supposes they got the idea from the exterminator brochures. *Most people have forgotten what it was like*, thinks Sonja, remembering the color of the moss among the ranks of fir. The dry stones, the grass, the gravel roads. The bald tires and silage. The sweet smell of silage, yes, and the dead piglets on the manure pile. Chickens with gizzards full of grit. Round bales in the rain, and there were hideouts everywhere and with them kids, and down at Super Aage's you'd often find his wife behind the counter. She'd stand there and snoop in people's purchases. She interpreted what was in the shopping carts according to signs and counsel, and she knew who was having their period. She knew who'd stopped having periods. Who drank.

Who put too much gelatin in the lemon mousse. Smoking habits, crossword preferences. The woman knew everything, and she wouldn't give kids credit on sweets. You could have any piece of candy in the world for just 5 øre, but she didn't do charity, and Sonja remembers Kate standing outside the store, waiting for the bus. Kate, standing over by the bus stop in new jeans. Her ass has always looked good in tight pants. She's standing with Bacon Bjarne, even though he wouldn't be called that till later. She sleeps with him twice a week. She's said so herself, and Sonja believes it, for she's heard them in the attic. Now they're standing at the bus stop with fingers interlaced. Kate can't be more than fifteen, but she doesn't have time to waste, and Sonja's standing there with her bike. Perhaps it's Saturday. They have no plans. Or rather, Sonja's got no plans, and then the bus comes. Bjarne and Kate vanish on board, and Sonja bikes out of Balling, heading home. She bikes the route she usually bikes after school. It's a boring route to bike. Sonja pretends that she can't look anywhere except right in front of the wheel. She rides along with her gaze drilling down into the pavement. It's fascinating how long she dares to. The bike tire whirrs, the spokes flash. Sonja can hear the clatter of the chain. There are birds chirping, and farm machinery. Sonja's eyes are shackled to the point in front of the wheel. She wants to bike like this the entire way home. It's a kind of bravery, but then suddenly it's there, by the viaduct: the car, parked on the shoulder. Sonja slams bang into it. She strikes the rear of the car and flies over her handlebars. She lands halfway across the trunk. The first thing she thinks is that you should never destroy other people's property. The second thing she thinks is that it hurts. Then she hears someone laughing. Two men and a woman are standing on the shoulder. It's the couple who live in the house by the viaduct and a man Sonja doesn't know. They laugh and say funny things while they lift up Sonja's bike. There's blood on her hand, and the wife asks about it briefly, but shame propels Sonja back up on her bike. She rides home with one hand on the handlebars, down the gravel driveway, into the farmyard, into the hallway, nobody home, outside again and into the rye, deep into the rye, and there she lays herself down with her hand raised. Cries.

Sonja's crying now. She's sitting in the window and looking at the manufactured owls. She doesn't understand the weeping, but a vision of Kate's ass by the bus clings doggedly to it. *A kind of happiness in passing*, Sonja thinks, and she tears off a paper towel. *Kate got everything she wanted*, Sonja thinks, *and in the order she wanted it. Kate's never colored outside the lines*, she thinks, for now she feels sorry for herself. The weeping feels like concern, and the concern reaches her belly. It loosens her jaw, and it's nice in a way, so it's welcome to continue. But then it can't continue anyway. Sonja runs dry, and now she's sitting there in the window and weighing whether to go over and lie in the cemetery. A pair of sunglasses, a blanket, then just head over to the cemetery and lie down. *But over there it's the same old grind*, thinks Sonja, and she looks at her hand. An ordinary hand, a woman's hand. You can't tell by looking at it that it had once been broken.

11.

Dear Kate,

So I'm going to try a letter anyway. Don't let that confuse you. I've got to spend the time doing something, ha-ha! The other day, I was out driving with my new instructor and we got to talking about Bjarne—you know, Bacon Bjarne. It's weird that he bought the family farm. He slapped you, back when you broke up with him. I'm sure we all remember that, but I know—it's so long ago now, and Bjarne always did have a sensitive ego. Yet to have to sniff the shite from the neighborhood asshole every day, Kate, and then put a brave face on it—that takes grit. For Frank too. That is, if he knows about the two of you. Over here, the big thing is to find your market segment and blend in, to not stand out, to become a chameleon and then flee all other social relations. I miss sticking by someone. Like a burr. I want to be as unshakable as kin, for over here it's all teflon, and I'm sorry I said that about the dead landscape up at Bjarne's. It's just that you're my sister . . .

Sonja fills both sides of the paper. Now she has to decide if it's worth bending down and fishing a fresh sheet out of the printer. She could have written a postcard. That would have created a natural limit. There were four postcards of heather in the discount pack. But maybe it doesn't matter; Sonja won't ever send what she's written, so there's no reason to waste postcards. *Suddenly I might have to attend a party*, she thinks, *and then of course I'll stand there needing a card. Even if no one throws parties anymore.* In Copenhagen, the parties have turned into receptions. People in stilettos and loafers, with wine and toothpicked hors d'oeuvres, stumbling around and having negligible conversations with each other. Their mouths pointing one way while their eyes are already sidling over to the next little group. And though the guests all belong to the same segment, which makes conversation cookie cutter, there's hierarchy in that hooey, and Kate wouldn't understand how that kind of thing grinds a person down.

The window's open. It's hot, much too hot. Something lies smoldering on the horizon, not really aspiring to anything. In a little while, the letter to Kate will be lying in the wastepaper basket. Mostly it's a question of flushing things from your system. As long as they remain in your body, they generate confusion. Ellen would understand that, and maybe Molly too.

Sonja writes some more on the letter. She takes a new sheet of paper and adds a couple of scenes from her daily life, a couple of comments about Mom and Dad, then ends by repeating that it makes her sad that she and Kate don't talk anymore. *Hugs & affection, your sister.*

Sonja regards the letter and wonders how well Kate remembers that she broke up with Bjarne during a country fair, or that he was pickled, which led to her getting that slap behind the clubhouse. That was it, a limp slap. Not enough to give her a shiner or anything, just the sort of thing that Sonja supposes any love life brings in its train. Only the gods know what people put up with over the years, but when Kate's home alone, there are too many such things haunting the crawl space. They're not easy to live with, day in, day out, and her irrational fears drive Frank up into the turbines. It drives him into planes bound for Africa, and then he stands there feeling lonely. He could sit down among the baobabs with his canteen, yes, he could sit down and sing. He could find himself, there on the savannah, but Kate's packed his bags with clean underwear and a dread of Ebola. Ebola, malaria, avian flu. So fear dwells cheek by jowl with Frank in his safari tent, though Kate wouldn't have it any other way. That the past contains stones we can use to build a bridge to a better future—Kate doesn't buy it. *And that's probably just fine*, Sonja thinks, *since the compulsion of ordinary people to remember every detail didn't really catch on until Ellen and Molly turned up.* Then it was all supposed to come out: the bloody hangnails, the botched intimate shave. The gingivitis, the cramps, the fear of insufficiency, the limp beery slaps and concomitant shiners—the whole kit and caboodle. Out into the light with that dreck! Out with it!

But who is Sonja to preach? Sonja, who can't recall what the woman in the curry tunic promised her in the way of misfortune as she stood leaning against the fridge. If you don't believe in the occult, you can't guard against it, Sonja realizes. And if you do believe, you're in deep shit, and how could Mom and Dad actually let him buy the farm, Bacon Bjarne? How pragmatic are people allowed to be? For if you swallow it all you're going to explode in the end, and she recalls the piglets that broke out of their sty once and got into the feed concentrate: how they lay out there on the walkway in the barn like dead little time bombs. But those days are gone. The piglets no longer escape from their sties, and apartment blocks are sprouting up in Sonja's vista like Lego bricks. The S-train croons underground, and she feels pain in her hip, her neck, the joint of her shoulder.

What I need is action, Sonja thinks. *I need something that pokes up from the horizontal. Some buoyancy, some catastrophe.*

Sonja opens the drawer. In it nestles the dust jacket from Gösta's last book, and under the dust jacket lie the envelopes. Sonja takes one and writes Kate and Frank's address on it. She has the address in her head, and then it's into the envelope with the letter she's written. On with the postage. It moves quickly from A4 sheet to potential catastrophe. *Buoyancy*, thinks Sonja. *Action!*

It's only when she's standing in the shopping center a short while later, pondering what to have for supper, that she comes to her senses. She can't send that letter. And it's not because of the business with Bjarne. It's the *way* Sonja expresses herself—indeed, the letter's very tone will interpose new distances between her and Kate. Like the time with the dead landscape between the equipment shed and the piggery. The time with the Devil and the absent chickens, and that's the problem: the things Sonja says *and* the way she says them.

Sonja can't stop smiling. The sizzle in her words frees up her jaw, and out in front of the clothing store for plus-size women, someone's parked a child. The child's sitting in a stroller, and its mother's begun to look at big clothes. The kid, who can't be more than three, has a bag of raisin buns that it's been plowing through. It's got bun sticking to its face and especially its fingers. Bun clings to the small creature, and some sort of cold is present as well. The kid's been commixing crumbs and raisin gook with oronasal secretions. It sounds as if it can't breathe on account of snot and pastry. Somewhere over by the store entrance, the mom's stuck her head down into a bin with king-size lingerie, and somewhere in Sonja's vicinity, the child freezes with a bun at mouth level. It has caught sight of Sonja and is staring at her, just like Sonja's staring at it. There's no sense in claiming it's a pretty child. But Sonja can't shake the memory of the piglets on the walkway in the barn. How they lay toppled there with their white distended bellies. How they were dead; how Sonja couldn't make them alive again. She asked her father if they couldn't find a way to bring them back to life. Since death was frightening, and she didn't understand the meaning of *forever.* She was begging him to cover up the truth, but Dad said there was nothing they could do. Time only moved forward. "They'll just have to go into the ground," he said. But it wasn't true; they didn't go into the ground. They were just dumped onto the manure pile, and over a long period of time Sonja witnessed how white turned to black, and how a couple of them ended up in fact exploding, and it was fascinating, unbearable. The piglets had done something stupid by gorging on concentrate. But the consequences of this minor mistake were terrible, and it was a short time later that she wheedled her way into Indre Mission, *but that didn't help*, thinks Sonja, and now she walks over to the child. She squats down beside it. The two of them are screened by a rack of clothing, sizes L to XXXXL, and the child's bun hesitates at its mouth.

"Did someone get some raisin buns?"

The child's eyes skitter around for its mother.

"That's a mighty big bag anyway."

The child flings itself backward to catch a glimpse of its mother.

Sonja whispers, "Watch out you don't eat too many," and then she stands upright and glances over at the mother.

"Quite the little sweetheart you have here," she tells her.

The mother smiles and says thank you.

"Pretty too," Sonja says.

12.

SONJA'S LYING DOWN, her feet sticking out over the end of the table. She's naked except for her panties, and she gives herself props for actually turning up. After the business out in the deer park, she could have easily chosen to play ostrich. It would have been much simpler to change masseuses than to show up today with that knot in her right shoulder. But take away the interpretive zeal and Ellen's a brilliant masseuse.

"I simply couldn't find you guys again," says Sonja.

"Couldn't you just have peed behind a tree?" asks Ellen.

"I suppose so. But then it started to thunder and I've got a problem with peeing outside. I can't do it anymore, I'm too scared of being caught."

Sonja sends a thought to Balling's dogs, to its dogs and their owners. If your dog had an accident, you would normally rub its nose in it. You wanted to teach it a lesson and keep it from a repeat offense. But the teaching method also rubbed off on those who witnessed it, and Sonja's noticed of late how she checks the lock twice when using a strange bathroom. From fear of someone suddenly opening the door. Of them seeing her squatting there, in the middle of her accident. Truth be told, she prefers trees and bushes, but she can't tell Ellen that. Not now.

"Once I was in Jutland on the edge of a lake," Sonja tells her. "I was at this convent, working on something of Gösta's, but most of the time I lay on a dock and read poems on the sly. But then this one time I had to pee, and it was a long way up to the restrooms. There's this path that runs along the shore, where people take their Sunday strolls, but there wasn't anyone on it just then. So I decided to squat behind this little boat shed and pee with my back to the path. Then I squatted there, and boy did I have to pee. I couldn't finish, and Jutlanders are stealthy when they're on a stroll. Especially if they're golden oldies, and that's who came along then. I wasn't able to stop peeing, but there was nothing wrong with my reflexes, I pulled up my panties and took a step forward and nearly fell into the lake, which happened to be one of Denmark's deepest. It was just like a Norwegian fjord, it got ice cold a mere inch under the surface before going on down for another hundred feet of murk and mire."

Sonja can't see Ellen, but she can hear that she's smiling.

"So you could say I have a pee trauma," Sonja adds, and then Ellen laughs.

Finally. That's good, that's dandy. Now they're on the same side again—the side of laughter and massage. Sonja flatters herself that she can feel it in the way Ellen's hands stroke her back, and how they go down into the shoulder joint. Which is tense.

"Any clue how you got so stiff in the shoulder?" Ellen asks.

"Probably because I changed driving instructors."

Ellen's over the moon. She squeezes both Sonja's shoulders and says she considers the change of instructors a breakthrough in Sonja's treatment.

Her treatment?

"Actually, I've been thinking that it's a step forward too," Sonja says. "Even though Jytte's still at the school, you know, and my new driving instructor . . ."

It seems to Sonja that, in the floor's knotty landscape, Mickey Mouse is moving. It's that dog again. He's supposed to come when called, but he won't.

"Yes? What's up with the new instructor?"

"Nothing, except that of course he's supposed to teach me how to shift gears, and when he taught me last time, he had to hold my hand."

Even though you're usually supposed to read something into everything at Ellen's, Ellen tells her that she shouldn't read anything into it.

"But I'm confused about my role as student," Sonja says. "Apart from the sexual subtext, Folke's not quite your run-of-the-mill driving instructor."

"Do you like him?" asks Ellen, rubbing vigorously.

"I like that he's his own man," says Sonja. "The rest of him interests me very little."

"But what about your love life? If I may be so bold."

In fact, that's something Ellen may *not* be. *Besides*, Sonja thinks, *you're one to talk. You don't look like someone who's being waited on hand and foot. That gaze of yours, those cosmic escape attempts—it's obvious you're hungry, and there's nothing you'd like better than to be bedazzled and swept away. And people in glass houses . . .* That's what Sonja thinks, and Molly's another one who's always on about other people's love lives. They ought to be like hers, ideally. But Molly's love life is chaotic, it's anxious and busy throwing a monkey wrench into the status quo, without letting the status quo get suspicious. There are periods when she has workers coming over all the time. The house belonging to Molly and the lawyer is always being overrun by workers—to say nothing of shamans and fortune tellers. These types let Molly cut corners in her life, while Molly's clients at the clinic are supposed to take the hard way. "To hell and back is good for the soul," Molly says, but she won't have any of it herself. Each time her existential angst threatens to suck her down into a childhood pool of sour whey, Molly gets carpenters to go over all the windows in Hørsholm. Plumbers, painters, and chimneysweeps for the practical bits, New Age drummers for the rest. Then the shadow theater's under control, but at night the curtain rises on a second act. Then Molly lies there, unable to remember her lines. She's sweating, and maybe it's anxiety, maybe it's menopause. In any case it's unpleasant, and so in the morning, when the lawyer's driven off to the office, she rings for a plumber, because then the faucet will work. It mustn't drip, no, and the heart-shaped face mustn't be spoiled, and now she's ready for clinic. The clinic's located in the basement of the Hørsholm house. The moment Molly steps over the threshold, she's filled with perspective and compassionate insight. She needn't go any farther than the driveway, where her rhododendrons lack the acidic soil they require for growth, for the madness to take hold, but in the clinic she has colored chalk, scented candles, and power over someone she thinks knows less.

"Don't you want to talk about it?" Ellen asks.

"About what? Where were we?"

"Your love life."

"Oh that," Sonja says, and then she doesn't say anything, and it might be that that confuses Ellen, but so be it.

In a lot of ways, thinks Sonja, *Mom did me a disservice in believing I could just be myself. If I hadn't been allowed to, then I'd be sitting right now with the whole package, but that train's left the station. And if anyone does, Mom should know that you have to adapt if you're going to entangle yourself in an intimate relationship. Kate knows that too. And Dad.*

Sonja looks down at the floor; she has no choice. She thinks of how Kate's always been good at toiling. Just like Ellen, she's busy making the lives of the disabled easier. She's got two large boys who've flown the nest. She's got a golden retriever and a membership in a gymnastics and fitness club. She bakes kringles and knits woolen stockings for Mom and Dad's old feet.

"You're tensing up," says Ellen.

"Am I?"

"What are you thinking about?"

"My sister, I think."

"Want to tell me about her?"

Sonja raises herself a bit on her elbows. It's her neck that's tensing, and she catches sight of one of Ellen's angels. This one's got a string around its neck and hangs dangling in the window.

"No, not really," Sonja says. "It was just that business with the gearstick. Have you ever tried driving a car in Jutland?"

Ellen has, and Sonja can see it before her: how good she is, at forward and reverse and parallel parking.

"Have you noticed, then, how they drive with their dicks?"

"What do you mean?"

"No really, they drive with their dicks. Like men: me first, me first, me first. The women too. Up on the ass of the driver in front of them, just perching there, waiting for there to be enough gap to squeeze through. On the long straight highways in Jutland, they drive in clumps with their bumpers a yard apart. There's plenty of room for all, but still they drive in these little cliques of mutual harassment. My nephews drive that way—with their dicks, that is. All the way forward, hanging and breathing on the necks of their fellow drivers. There are more traffic fatalities in Jutland than anywhere else in Denmark. My mom and I were once overtaken on a side road by a woman who apparently sold Tupperware. It said TUPPERWARE on the car that roared past us anyway. My mom had to pull over on the shoulder afterward to gather her wits. Does it actually bother you that I use words like that?"

"Like what?"

"Like *dick*, for instance."

"Use whatever words you want."

Fine, thinks Sonja, face to face with Mickey Mouse on the floorboards. *Dick and dick and dickety dick.*

It eases the joint of her jaw a bit when she makes herself vulgar. Coarse words are good for the mouth muscles, and she knows a slew of them too. She could let a torrent of filth gush forth in Ellen's clinic.

"I'm like my mom," says Sonja. "We've got these rich, expansive inner worlds. We're quite intelligent. But as women, we're not completely fine-tuned."

The massaging hands slacken off on her neck. It's as if she's said something that could make a pin drop. Like a bolt of lightning, it's driven all the air from the room, and Sonja lies there waiting for Ellen to throw herself into some interpretation. But she's evidently passing up the chance.

"So where at Bakken *were* you during the thunderstorm?"

Sonja leaves out The Blue Coffeepot and the musicians from Ballerup. Now she and Ellen are good friends again. Sonja doesn't need to add her wedge of cake to the mix. She doesn't know if she enjoyed herself at Bakken, but it was better than following Ellen into the deer park, for the deer park's not natural. The red deer are too tame, not like the huge herds that drifted across the far part of Dad's land. They found their way into the root cellars, and it was good to sit out there and watch them ruminate. Their large ears, their gazelle nature, and what a winter's day to walk among the firs. To wander as far out upon the heath as possible. Someplace out there, the whooper swans were alighting. The yellow bills, the long white necks, and, somewhere on the periphery, Dad's deer stand awaits like a giant empty high-chair.

It was a landscape full of power, Sonja thinks. *Dad would sit there under the pretext of wanting to hunt. I'd sit there because it was the best place to be myself. But we both wanted the same thing. When you overcame the anxiety, and the boredom, you were alive there. Completely present. That's how it was for Dad, while Mom had that place inside her, and I wanted both: the innermost* and *the outermost.*

Sonja regards Ellen through half-open eyes. From this position, she can't see Ellen's face with its heavy eyes, only her midriff. Ellen probably doesn't realize it, but a quiet growling sound is coming from her throat. An agreeable sound, as she rubs away at Sonja, and aside from Sonja's body it's that power, the one you'd find in the farthest part, that Ellen wants to sink her fingers into. But you don't find that sort of thing in a deer park. *The name alone!* thinks Sonja, and it isn't something she could explain to Ellen. How would she know that some phenomena require an emptiness, a wilderness, a stillness in which people do not exist?

"How'd it go with your meditation?" Sonja ventures.

"We hid in a small thicket," says Ellen.

"You see any stags?"

"Aren't stags the big ones?" asks Ellen.

They are, and now Sonja has to flip onto her back. Every time she flips on her back, Ellen starts talking about her dizziness as something psychosomatic.

"It's a case of imbalance."

"There is that, yes," says Sonja.

"And the imbalance has its origin in something spiritual. There's something in your life that's whirling around. Something that doesn't know how to manifest itself."

"My doctor's more of the opinion that there are tiny stones in my ears that have to settle into place."

"But doctors are doctors, you know."

And stones are stones, thinks Sonja.

13.

Above Ellen's clinic in Valby, the sky has closed itself off. Sonja had been listening to the distant rumble while she lay on the massage table. Near the end she let herself doze off, but now she's on her feet again.

"It's like trying to breathe underwater," Ellen says, and she suggests that Sonja stay and drink tea until it passes over.

But Ellen's cat has entered the picture. The cat's almost twenty years old and its coat is tufty, its gaze sallow. It must be some kind of Persian. It's flat in the face, anyway, and sometimes when Sonja swings her legs over the edge of the table, it'll be sitting in the doorway, staring at her. Sonja likes cats. The affectionate and playful ones, that is, but while dogs mirror their owners' essence, Sonja doesn't dare to think what this cat might represent.

"It's getting on in years," Sonja says out in the hall.

"Yeah, and things are going to start going downhill pretty soon," Ellen says, looking worriedly at the cat, which is tottering at their heels. Then Ellen repeats her offer of a cup of tea. "I'd like to tell you about going to the States. To Southern California."

A light that Sonja hasn't seen before goes on in Ellen's face. Like a Christmas tree in the darkness of December.

"California?" asks Sonja.

"California, yes!"

Ellen shelves all talk of tea, and now she's telling Sonja that she and Anita from the deer park are going to San Diego. They're going to see this woman with medical intuition. She's famous, because she can tell what's wrong with a person just by looking at them. But not only that; she can also tell why the person's suffering from what they're suffering. She's especially good at finding the psychological causes of breast cancer.

"If a woman doesn't talk about stuff, it settles in her breasts."

"But women tend to talk about stuff a lot," says Sonja.

"The important stuff. Emotional life, sexuality. Relationships with their mothers and fathers. With kids and boyfriends."

"With everything?"

"Yes, you could say that."

Sonja can't avoid thinking about Kate and the stamped envelope in her bag. Never in her life would she send it. She just pretends that she could, but the notion that *not* wanting to send the letter might have an effect on the development of breast cancer makes the atmosphere sticky. There's also something muddy in the cat's gaze.

"This intuitive woman works with the relationship between life stories and case histories. We have to get things out in the open. Out of the body, all of it."

Ellen's making dismissive gestures with her hands. She does that frequently. As if the bad things within us could be cast away if only we could grasp them with our hands. Yes, if only they were graspable.

"I once talked to a fortune teller," Sonja says without really wanting to.

"Really?" says Ellen, brightening up.

"Yes, I didn't believe what she said of course, but then I began to believe anyway, because—well, because I was worried about the future, and because I have the sense that she promised me that I *had* one. In fact I can't remember what she said. I've repressed it, I think."

A star appears on the top of Ellen's inner Christmas tree; she smells of fir, light green. Sonja's going to let her inside now; they're going to share this.

"That sounds significant," Ellen whispers.

"Maybe," says Sonja. "She said in any case that I'd be unlucky in love, and then I was. But I've forgotten the rest. Sometimes at night I'm afraid she said something terrible, and that's why I can't remember it. And then other times, I'm anxious that she might have said something marvelous, and that it's dangerous to remember because then it won't happen. I don't believe in fortune-telling. Not at all. But if you don't believe in the occult, you can't guard against it. It's a strange paradox. Almost a catch-22."

Ellen leans her face in toward Sonja's.

"The seeress is an ancient figure," she says.

The cat attempts to drape herself around Ellen's foot. It's an ancient figure too, and now there's definitely a booming in the distance.

"Yes, but it's such a long journey," says Sonja. "To San Diego, I mean. I imagine you'll take a little time to look around while you're there?"

"We leave on Friday and fly back Sunday evening."

Sonja's obviously not quite getting this.

"Meaning a bit more than a week?"

"No, from Friday to Sunday."

"You're going to San Diego for a long weekend?"

"Yes."

Sonja doesn't know what to say. She doesn't need to say anything either. Judging by her expression, Ellen knows this is utter madness.

"If you're really passionate about something, you have to seize the chance," she says.

To illustrate, Ellen sticks her hand out and squeezes Sonja's upper arm. Sonja doesn't care for this contact and has an urge to yank back her arm, to defend herself.

"But three days?" Sonja asks, and she rubs her arm where Ellen's released it.

"If you're really passionate about something, you seize the chance," Ellen says again, and Sonja takes a small step back toward the doorframe. She's afraid that Ellen will take it into her head to throw her arms around Sonja and pull her into an embrace. She's afraid of the light in Ellen's eyes, the door behind her that might spring open any moment and reveal how things actually stand, and Sonja really doesn't know her. She doesn't want to know her either. She wants to have Ellen's powerful hands on her, not around her, no, she doesn't want to be captured, and she manages to avoid being touched again. Instead, Ellen's telling her how, by placing people in a circle around her, the medically intuitive woman can see the future in their connective tissue.

"See the future?"

"Yes. Connective tissue is a kind of network that weaves in and out between all your organs, bones, and joints. The connective tissue *connects* everything. They've discovered that connective tissue can resist cancer cells, even though cancer always *starts* in the connective tissue. It's got that strange duality, but that's only because it's also connected to spiritual conditions. The connective tissue's like a sheet of paper where we write down everything that's unsayable, and then it develops into cancer for instance. Traumas reside in the connective tissue; they never leave the body. And when you get dizzy for example, it's because your connective tissue is trying to tell you something."

An intriguing theory, thinks Sonja, holding her breath as Ellen's eyes look searchingly at her. Sonja's supposed to let herself be carried along. Then they can rise from the ground together, and maybe Ellen's just as capable of crying as she is of standing there lighting up. Sonja doesn't know, she only knows she doesn't want to be involved. She's not paying four hundred crowns an hour to be involved.

Sonja grasps the doorknob. The relief she got from saying *dick* on the massage table has dissipated; her jaw's tense again.

"Medical intuition's the future," Ellen says. "Modern medicine is bankrupt."

Sonja glances down at Ellen's cat. It looks like the seed head of a cattail that someone's begun to pluck the down from.

"So now Anita and I are taking off," Ellen adds, following Sonja halfway out the door. "I'm telling you this only because you won't be able to come to massage next week."

It's rumbling over Valby, and Ellen's inner Christmas tree has burst into flame. Sonja says that, thunder or no thunder, she's got to get biking. Ellen can't persuade her to have a cup of tea, no. They take their leave out on the patio, Sonja wishing her happy trails, and a moment later she's on her bike. She's still in the residential area when the first drops fall. A short time later the sky lashes out, and a vast exchange commences between the earth and sky.

14.

THERE'S A SPOT among the fashionable boulevards of Ellen's neighborhood where someone's erected a shelter. Inside the shelter is a bench. The idea is for locals to sit there and share a cold one. But the sort of locals who'd like to sit in the open with a cold one can't afford this neighborhood, so they live elsewhere. Sonja's bike leans up against the shelter while she sits within, listening to the thunder.

Medical intuition and cosmic forces, she thinks, feeling a tad soiled. As if she'd gone home with a charlatan, yes, as if loneliness had made her a salesman's easy mark. A trace of incense is clinging to her, but it might as well be Magic Tree air freshener, bad cologne, a backseat blanket, and gunk between her thighs.

San Diego?

The things that drive people.

That shaman that Molly ran around with for a while, the Belgian, was as white and spindly as a tapeworm and nearly as voracious. He trotted around Hareskoven, beating on drums and tossing sage around. The son of a civil servant in Brussels, yet utterly capable of casting a curse in the Danish suburbs. *A narrow margin of uncertainty about the true nature of everything can create all manner of anxiety in the world*, thinks Sonja, for Molly wanted the shaman to take her from behind. He should come when she called and take her for a good canter. The lawyer might be a good father, but Molly was more into magic pokers. It was passion, she'd claim at the time, and yet she'd grow fearful when she broke it off. Then she'd hasp the windows tight, or sit with Sonja at a café and whimper. She'd wonder how the shaman could have seduced her. Her, a psychologist, and Sonja found it peculiar as well. *Yet who am I to judge*, thinks Sonja, recollecting the fortune teller's curry-yellow presence in Molly's kitchen.

I wish I could remember my future, she thinks. *But I also wish I could forget that she gave me one. If she did give me one.*

The heavens thunder and lighten. One strike after another, rolling in from the south. The rain hammers the asphalt, and the more it rains, the more Sonja's sense of discomfort from over at Ellen's dissipates.

Thunder's a good thing. While Mom sat with her and drank thunder joe up in the dormer window, Dad preferred to run around down in the living room. He'd pull the plugs from the TV equipment and make sure to keep away from windows. It was no good to put him out in the car and assure him it was safe. "I'm still in contact with the ground," he'd say. That four radial tires stood between him and the big shock meant nothing to his intellect. In Dad's head, he was always touching the ground. If they were lucky, Mom and Sonja, and he wasn't home when there was lightning, they'd shuck off their shoes. Then they'd wade around in the pond that the rain formed in the courtyard while Kate screamed at them to get out.

It's strange, actually, that we dared to, thinks Sonja now. *As if we couldn't die from that sort of thing, but then of course we didn't die.*

There's a buzzing in her body. Small packets of endorphins being released; it's the massage taking root in her from within. Her right shoulder is warm and alive. The pain's still there, but it feels warm and alive. Like when blood floods back into a frozen hand, and the sky's doing it too: it tumbles down. When it rains this hard, she can't see the city she's gone astray in. Nor can she hear it. The inhabitants have vanished, the cars have pulled over. People sit in their kitchens and fear for their basements. They stand and peer out from under awnings.

Sonja pushes her shoes off and stretches her long legs. It feels good to take off her moccasins. She thinks of love, for Paul's still a living part of her awareness. What he could do to her with his face, now she thinks back on it. He had an effect, Paul did, but if it weren't that Sonja had such a hard time forgetting everything—except her future, that's gone—the effect wouldn't have lasted so long.

Back in Balling, you screwed whatever was at hand. You weren't going anywhere, after all. You had to take from the assortment available, and it wasn't very large. But you learned to make do, and you learned to tolerate. And hang in there. Just not Sonja.

Once when Sonja was sixteen, Kate told her that she should give things time. That she should keep going out with Kenneth. Kenneth didn't have anything against tall girls, and she didn't need to be in love with a guy to begin with. If she gave it time, the feelings would grow on her. Like moss, almost, or yeast cells. They'd multiply, in any case, because the two of them would became entangled in each other. Because the world around them grew accustomed to the constellation. It might well be that the role was as flat as a pancake, but it demanded no effort, other than to keep dancing slow dances with Kenneth. To keep feeling Kenneth's tongue in her oral cavity. To let Kenneth stick his hand into her panties and press up with his fingers. That's what you did: choose or make sure you're chosen. When the situation settled down, the cow would no longer be out on the ice and everyone could breathe easy. No longer were you a potential misfit or a traitor to your class.

But then Kenneth invited Sonja to the movies to see Jodie Foster in *The Accused*, and Sonja had already seen it. Kate thought that that didn't matter, the whole idea was getting the pot to boil. But Sonja had seen *The Accused* and knew that five or six men would take turns raping Jodie Foster over the same kind of pinball machine that they had in the sports clubhouse. Sonja didn't care to subject their relationship to that, so she let Kenneth stand and wait in vain in front of the movie theater. He was five foot six and the youngest son from the plant nursery. A nice boy. Good with animals, and of course Kate didn't get it at all. She felt that Sonja had sinned against the M.O.

Yet staying away from Kenneth was the smartest thing I've done in my so-called love life, thinks Sonja, while the heavens flash and bang overhead. *And then there was the time that that guy Tonny, the one Marie married, had stood in the back passage over at Kate and Frank's, and we'd been barbecuing, and folks had gotten pretty pixilated, and then he'd pulled out his prick.*

He'd stood over by Kate's dryer and asked, "Don't you want to put it in your mouth?" and he looked like Mickey Mouse, yes, like Mickey Mouse with those big ears, though his prick looked more like a tulip. A cut white tulip when it starts to swell and open. And while there's a certain power in being always willing to take a prick in your mouth, you shouldn't underestimate the power of not being willing to take a prick in your mouth.

Sonja draws in her feet. She goes over her string of men. The list isn't terribly impressive, but it's left its mark nonetheless. Like cheap sex itself. Lean meat, lanolin, the taste of rubber. Palle Mikkelborg and the shower stalls, and later there came early adulthood's attempts at conversion and retention. First the married college adjunct, and then the composer, but he drank, and how Sonja got the notion that she could convert first a narcissist and then an alcoholic seems incomprehensible as she sits here now, free of her moccasins. Not to forget the period with newly divorced men. For instance Paul.

He'd been there at the convent, the one with the psychic chambermaid in faraway Jutland. It was early in the morning, and the first thing Sonja saw was the light in his face. *So there we have him*, she'd thought: *the unhappy love.*

Paul claimed that he'd seen the ghost in room 10. He'd been lying there in bed, unable to sleep. The sounds from the highway fled across the heath. It was as if the landscape around him became young again. He's been looking at the desk when a mist arose. The mist came toward him as he lay there in bed, and he'd had to sit up in order to see her. For it was a woman. "I don't dare sleep in room 10 again now," he'd said. "Where are you sleeping?"

Sonja was in room 7 and thought the ghost had been a man with a hipster goatee. Paul said she was mistaken. "The ghost is a woman—not unlike you."

And then part of Sonja felt suspiciously light-headed, and part of her felt that she might as well get the unhappy affair over with. So she could move on with her life. After it was over, that is. She'd smiled, and Paul had automatically turned up the volume in his face. He let warmth stream out of its orifices, and Sonja didn't twig that she was the target of a trick. She thought *she* was the one who'd inspired the warmth in Paul's face. But there she was mistaken, for nature wants woman to offer up her body, and Sonja certainly saw the signs. After all, it wasn't as if Paul hid his attraction for Gitte Hænning when she'd been a teen sensation. Wasn't as if he didn't sign his letters with arch aliases. *Love, Paul Pedant,* he wrote; he wrote *Love, Miss O'Gyne.*

But Sonja had to go through with the unhappy infatuation. It was tough, and now she can't walk past faces that light up too much, jack-o'-lanterns for instance, without thinking of Paul the Ex. Paul and that twenty-something girl he preferred in reality. The type who could look up to him and wanted to marry Daddy.

I've got an unfortunate tendency to love men who can't really see me, Sonja thinks. *They can't see me, but I'm such a fighter, Mom says. She says I can make anything happen. Yet "I can't make you love me,"* Sonja thinks, and then she can't remember who it was who sang that song. She has to dig her phone out of her shorts pocket. She does a quick search for info. Bonnie Raitt, bingo, but now Sonja's forgotten: what was she just thinking? She can't find her way back, it's sealed itself off, and the rainwater slides along the asphalt in waves. *It won't be long before the rats arrive,* she thinks. When the water rises in the sewers, they swim upward. When the water fills the sewers, the rats make their way toward the manhole covers. When the water gets that high, the rats drown, and that's a good thing. Yeah, that's a good thing.

15.

IF YOU DRIVE FAR ENOUGH SOUTH from Balling, down toward the Skjern River and out toward Ringkøbing Fjord, you come upon a heath. It was down there on the fringe that Mom was born, and the heath was called Lønborg. She often told us that, unlike other heaths in Denmark, it had never been cultivated. It consisted chiefly of gravel and sand, and it was hard to get so much as a twig to sprout there. The heath had lain there for millennia, untouched by human hands—vast, eerie, and capricious. People would tell how they'd lost their way on the heath. They declared that they'd had fixed reference points in the landscape, but that the landscape was dynamic. It revolved, changed form, did whatever it wanted. Then when Mom was young, an American moved into the area. And he didn't fear the landscape. Every weekend he'd go out on the heath, come rain, come shine, and at regular intervals he'd go missing. His wife had to ring the police chief several times, though her husband always did turn up. Then she'd chew him out for not looking after himself. But he did: the American tied ribbons to dry branches and chalked crosses on stones, although on the heath such markers tended to move. "Time and space behave differently out there," the American maintained, and he knew what he was talking about, because in the US they had pristine landscapes of such immensity and abundance that they developed consciousnesses of their own. Everyone there knew that the prairies, the mountains, and the deep forests all have their own characters. "The laws we bow before are ones they rise above—or rather, ones they've never been subject to," the American said, declaring that such landscapes didn't give a fig about the minuscule consciousness of the human individual. The wilderness zigged right, zagged left, it rose and curved the way the universe curves. A tiny person alone would get discombobulated as the wilderness unspooled, and the tiny person would run around, searching for civilization. "But the American," said Mom, "he'd sit down on a stone out there, and he'd just kept sitting in that spot until the landscape settled and lay still. Then he'd walk home. Happy, he claimed, and our minister backed him up, even as he advised people to stay off the heath. There were forces out there that weren't to be trifled with, the minister said."

"What kind of forces, Mom?"

"Female forces, I expect," Mom said, and Sonja walked out into the farthest part.

She walked through the tree plantation onto open land and farther out, farther. She walked out to the whooper swans, and there she sat down like the American sat down on Lønborg Heath: she surrendered sovereignty, came to herself, put people behind her, and was happy there in her yellow clogs.

But Søndre Fasanvej slides into Frederiksberg. Soon Sonja has to get off the bus, and what if Jytte's standing there waiting in front of the driving school? What if she's standing there working up a rage? How do you hide from people who make themselves angry just to feel alive? They're everywhere, and it's tricky making yourself invisible in a world that's as flat as a pancake. Nervousness gropes Sonja from within. It's the drive with Folke, but it's also the fear of confrontation.

Sonja presses the STOP button and gets to her feet like an old woman. She's scared of getting dizzy and has to hold her head still, while at the same time bringing it with her. No tilting now. Down the bus steps, onto the city sidewalk, careful, careful. It's not because she's dizzy right now. It's because she mustn't become so. Sonja doesn't want to sit at Folke's side and not be in possession of her full five. His hands are diligent, his fingers long, and Sonja has books in her backpack. Now and then she'll squeeze in a historical romance in the breaks between Gösta, and perhaps Folke's wife has a taste for that kind of thing too, and it should seem as if his wife's sitting in the backseat.

Sonja moves through Frederiksberg on foot. She thinks of the letter that's still lying in her bag. Even though it'd be good for her connective tissue, she doesn't want to send it. She won't, no, and at the same time she's hoping that Jytte's out driving with somebody. Since Sonja began studying for her license, she's made special note of driving-school vehicles. This must be what it's like for mothers when they see other women with baby buggies. They're in the same boat. Like cells in a guerrilla movement, they don't need to put their reality into words. They can say everything with a look, no need for gesture. *Jytte could learn something from that,* Sonja thinks as she walks down Gammel Kongevej.

There are driving school vehicles at almost every light. Behind the wheel sit focused young folks. Once in a while Sonja glimpses an older person with shame in their face, but right now it's the seat with the instructor she's keeping an eye on.

Jytte?

No.

Jytte? Jytte—?

No.

Sonja turns onto Folke's street. It's a small street garnished with cars. Folke's vehicle is easy to spot. It looks like the sneaker of a towering basketball player, and Sonja doesn't feel safe approaching it. In the back of the car she can dimly see a figure poking up. The top of it is tinted henna, and it's emitting a plume.

Jytte?

Jytte.

She's gotten out of her Hyundai to smoke, and to judge from this distance, she's got approximately seven minutes of cigarette to burn. It may well be, as Folke claims, that Jytte has a heart of gold, but her heart's gotten a scratch, and here comes Sonja with her mutiny.

She's in the middle of life, Sonja, a grown woman, but she doesn't dare walk over past Jytte. Something in the situation makes her seize up so completely that she splits in two. She's someone who knows that the right thing would be to act like a grown-up, but she's also someone who would not for all the tea in China want to be confronted with her own treachery. It must have been a shock for Jytte when Folke told her that Sonja was somebody other than she'd feigned in the car. If she *was* feigning. Jytte did force Sonja into her world and presume she was part of it. It was as if she'd been hauled into Jytte's changing stall at the swimming pool, and there Jytte had shed all her clothes, peeling off her maxi panties while she spewed bile upon the planet's drivers. She involved Sonja in her family, and she revealed that she colored her ends.

Jytte had no doubt thought that, with all that intimate knowledge, Sonja couldn't possibly take flight. She'd been initiated, after all. And yet Sonja managed to squeeze her way out of the stall, and now Jytte's standing over there, belching smoke.

Gingerly, Sonja withdraws into a doorway. The doorway belongs to the local chess club, which is apparently open only during evening hours. When Sonja went to theory with Folke, she often glimpsed the chess players steaming up the worn-out windows. They were all men, and a number of them were decidedly tall. While she stood and fumbled with her bike lock, they'd emerge now and then to smoke in the twilight. Then they'd stand there, tall and thin on top, and discuss castling. There was something safe about them, Sonja felt. Something enclosing, benign, almost confidence-inspiring, but now it's morning. The premises appear deserted and Sonja's hidden herself in the doorway. Sooner or later Jytte's student will arrive, and when that happens the coast will be clear.

It's really a form of fear, she thinks. *It's irrational in any case. I've purchased an item in Folke's shop. And Jytte's a grown person; an educator, kind of. It's not right for me to be scared of her feelings.*

She cautiously pokes her head out of the doorway. On the far right-hand side of the scene she can now see Folke. He's placed himself on the steps over there. Folke and Jytte are talking together as if nothing had happened, and then a door opens behind Sonja.

"Excuse me, if I may?"

A man is standing in the stairwell, wanting to go out onto the street. A tall man. He looks like one of the chess players, skinny as a snake, but this fellow has a stroller with him. In the stroller, a toddler sits and sulks. The child doesn't want to go outside, and definitely doesn't want to go with him.

"Sure, of course," says Sonja, stepping quickly to the side.

The stroller charges over the doorsill. The chess player's irritated with the child, the child with the chess player. The child's acting haughty in the stroller, and the chess player tackles the front steps a bit too roughly. Then the child drops its teddy bear.

"I'll get it," says Sonja.

She bends quickly for the bear and instantly it's there: the positional vertigo.

It's an acute attack. It's the sort that makes her eyes centrifuge. Someplace in Sonja's head, a darkness descends and she has to grab for the chess player. She gets ahold of his elbow, latching on to it, otherwise out of control. Her body catapults and her mind swims, but in the middle of feeling she's lost her footing she manages to apologize.

"I'm just a little bit dizzy," she says.

"Don't you want to sit down?" the chess player asks.

"Yes, please," says Sonja, but it's a major attack.

She has a hard time getting herself seated without sailing into the brickwork. The chess player lets go of the stroller, Sonja grabs for his leg and then clings to him, and he clings to her, and she's about to cry. It arrives swiftly and unexpectedly.

This sensation of the chess player's jeans and behind them, the hard shinbone, the skin.

"Oh man," he says.

The stroller with the angry toddler starts rolling down the sidewalk, but the chess player's a modern man and he grabs the angry toddler with one hand while the other keeps its grip on Sonja. Somewhere in the distance, Jytte's grinding out her cigarette, but Sonja doesn't witness it. Her eyes are closed and confounded.

"Can you sit up now?"

"Yes," she says, leaning her head against the door behind her. "There, I just have to hold my head still for a bit."

"Are you sure you don't want to call somebody?" asks the chess player, who's evidently just a dad from the building.

Sonja's worlds slowly lay themselves over each other. Now she can see the man who's helped her. He's got discomfort painted on his face, a furious child in his stroller, and a woman around his ankle. Sonja releases him and the child screams. It doesn't *want* to, it wants to get out and down and in again. It has a strong will to not want to do anything, this child. Its mother is doubtless up in their apartment, and perhaps she's braided her hair and is sitting down with a cup of coffee. Or perhaps she's standing up there and looking out the window, at Sonja, at the sky, at the pigeons rising up in great flurries.

"Shouldn't I just call someone?"

The chess player has gotten his phone out.

"No, I just have to sit for a little while," says Sonja. "It's a condition called BPPV."

That's too many letters for the chess player.

"Otolithic vertigo," she tries.

Still too many letters.

"A family disorder."

The child, a boy Sonja can see now, has started to disintegrate. Tears leak out of every opening in his face, and he won't sit down.

"You probably need to get a raisin bun for him there," she says, pointing.

"If you don't think I should call anyone . . ."

"You shouldn't, you should just take care of him," she says, for whom should he call?

Ellen's hovering up in the air, Molly's drawing giraffes in her clinic, Kate isn't answering the phone and Mom and Dad are old. There's no one to ride to the rescue, and she's also feeling better now. Her long legs clatter onto the sidewalk. Her hands are resting in her lap, and she listens to the stroller squeaking down the street with the chess player's footfalls right behind.

"Thank you!" Sonja shouts after him, but there's no telling if he hears it as he rounds the corner.

She focuses on a bay window in the building across the street. In the window is a potted plant, and next to the plant is a birdcage. In the cage sits a bird, and the bird is yellow. It hangs by its beak, and maybe it isn't a bird. You can buy birds made of kapok that are stone dead from the get-go. *And now I've got a potential conflict with Folke*, Sonja thinks, for now she's late. She can't make the excuse that she got dizzy.

She can never ever tell Folke that she gets dizzy.

16.

JYTTE'S DRIVEN OFF, the coast is clear, and Sonja's seated herself cautiously in Folke's car. While Folke fusses with her driving school papers, she places her hand on the gearstick. She wants to be certain of where it is, for it's important not to look down too much while driving. She squeezes the head of the gearstick in her palm and goes over the gears' H-pattern. No diagonals, no diagonals. Then she feels Folke's hand on top of hers; it's warm, and he squeezes gently.

"In this shop, we show up on time."

A mild warmth flows from Folke's hand, but she's not sure she likes it. It makes her feel weak about the throat and no, she doesn't like it. In another context, perhaps, but she's paying to learn to drive, not to sit here and be intimate.

"Yes, I'm sorry about that," Sonja says while her hand scoots away from under Folke's like a flatfish beneath a flip-flop. "But I brought a few books for you. They're on the backseat. They're for your wife—you told me she likes to read."

Folke flips down his sunglasses and goes through Sonja's papers again. He also fishes a bag of gummy bears out of the passenger door. They're from a student who forgot their papers for a lesson. That's the rule: it costs a bag of Haribos if you forget. Sonja declines a bear, and it's only now with his mouth full of them that Folke twists around for the books. His bald pate's had some sun this weekend. It also looks like he's trimmed his beard. *So they must have been at the cottage*, thinks Sonja. *The foot doctor sitting there with Gösta, while Folke sat and gazed out across the ocean. He's the type who can sit and stare across an ocean for a long time*, Sonja thinks, as Folke pokes a finger into the book bag.

"You're looking a bit stiff," he says, and he leaves the books lying on the backseat.

"Crick in the neck."

Sonja's pushed back her seat. She's got her head in an upright position. *The next hour's all about not killing anyone*, she thinks. She just has to drive as quietly as possible. Turn your entire body when you look back at your blind spot, she tells herself, while Folke tells her that Thai massage is supposed to help. He's got that on Jytte's authority, because she drives with a Thai woman named Pakpao, and Pakpao's good at Thai massage. Sometimes Jytte gets this incredible pain in a spot right between her shoulder blades, and Pakpao doesn't always have enough money for lessons, so sometimes they turn off onto a side street.

"It might not be legal," Folke says, "but out here in the real world, we solve problems where they crop up."

Sonja focuses on a fixed point, an Aldi sign a bit farther down the street. If her world hadn't been reduced to the one commandment not to kill, perhaps she'd tell Folke that it can't be fair that Pakpao's *always* forced to pay in kind, but Sonja shall not kill, she shall not kill, and what business of hers is the back of Jytte's heart anyway?

"Today we're going to hit the highway," says Folke.

Sonja stares at the Aldi sign. Then her gaze drifts with a blue patch of sky across the roofs of Frederiksberg's buildings.

"We're going to go out and give it some oats," says Folke.

Sonja's tried driving on the freeway before, that's not the problem. She likes the fact that freeways are straight, and that's especially good news today. But she also knows that they're full of blind spots. She and Jytte once drove the stretch between Folehaven and Vallensbæk, and Sonja hasn't forgotten the feeling of suicide every time Jytte yelled, "Change lanes goddammit, turleff, TURLEFF!"

"But I've only gotten to fourth gear," says Sonja.

"And today we'll get to fifth, maybe even sixth," says Folke, rubbing his hands together.

As if he wished to warm them up.

Sonja starts the car, and she looks back in her blind spot by twisting her entire upper body. Her head for God's sake must not rotate on its own.

"A smaller turn would do the trick just fine," says Folke.

"Yes, but there's no harm in being thorough," says Sonja, who's feeling anxious.

No, it's fear. It sings in her ears. The tiny stones have torn free inside. They scud about in dingy fluid like the snow in a globe from Himmelbjerget, and once Sonja bought just such a snow globe. It was on a trip to Himmelbjerget in third grade. Dad didn't think she should have any money along on the trip. "Surely not at that age," he said, but when he wasn't looking, Mom put some money in Sonja's pocket. "Buy something on Himmelbjerget," she said, and then Sonja bought a snow globe with the paddleboat *Hjejlen* inside. It stood inside a cabinet so that Kate couldn't see it.

Or Dad. But sometimes before she fell asleep, Sonja would take out the snow globe and give it a good shake. Then the tiny white flakes fluttered around in the viscous liquid. *Hjejlen* was moored in Lake Jul, and around Lake Jul the beeches were always in leaf. But then the snow squall would come, and a storm of dandruff would settle over the landscape. It was nothing special, yet still there was something in the metamorphosis that Sonja loved, and then last winter she was in Stockholm. A Gösta seminar, where Gösta was supposed to tell people how his books should be translated. And as if that wasn't enough, he'd also wanted to tell them how the books should be written, and at one point he told them that the crime commissioner ought to have a quirk. *Kvørk* is how Gösta said it. The commissioner ought to have a *kvørk*, an idiosyncratic penchant for chewing matchsticks or collecting toy cars. On top of his *kvørk*, the commissioner ought to drink and have family problems, preferably with a daughter. And like a good father, Gösta was sharing this sort of thing with his translators, translators who covered large swaths of Europe. Most of these translators had been educated at venerable universities, but the knowledge they'd acquired there was of no use anymore. During their lunches, Gösta told them about the house on Gotland, the picture windows, and the prospect out onto the real Sweden. They were long days, so in the evenings, Sonja would walk around the old city center. There in a window she saw a display of snow globes, big ones. Inside the globes there were castles, and landscapes of majesty such as you would only encounter in America. Sonja stood arrested before the shop window. She laid her forehead against the glass. How her hands yearned to touch the spheres, to take them home, keep them secret in her cabinet. To shake them. Yes, to shake them and ascertain that reality could turn into fairy tale with just a little jiggling.

Or into nightmare, thinks Sonja at the stoplight she's pulled up to. The light is red, and in a moment she'll proceed. Out onto the freeway with her absence of body, and Folke's hands.

"Nope, it's no picnic having a crick in your neck like that," he says.

"It comes and goes," says Sonja. "It's the deskwork," she says, and the light turns green.

Sonja drives slowly in the direction of the nearest on ramp. She says again that the stiffness in her neck is due to her work posture. Then she hasn't said too much, hasn't said too little. It's best that Folke knows to be extra attentive on her behalf, now when they're about to head out into southbound traffic.

"I'm not very good at Thai massage," says Folke, "but if you'd like me to rub anywhere, just say the word."

No doubt this is just the way he is, but it makes Sonja press down on the accelerator, because now they're going to drive toward Køge. It has to be gotten over with, and she's scared, and Folke senses that and tells her she shouldn't be. They've been spared the worst of the morning traffic, and besides, rush hour doesn't really pose a problem anyhow. You just have to drive against the traffic. Going *with* rush hour traffic is hell on wheels. Going *against* rush hour traffic is no trouble. "The drivers are like salmon in a river," Folke says. Køge lies someplace on the horizon of a wild fauna, and now they're on the entrance ramp. Now's when it starts, the great journey. Sonja doesn't want to think like that, but it's tough in traffic not to think of death.

"Would you change gears for me please?" Sonja hears herself asking.

"Fiddlesticks," says Folke, taking her hand again. "Clutch in, fourth . . . Fifth . . . And *voilà*, sixth. And you're going to just stay in this lane. No passing any eighteen-wheelers. Just stay here and keep it at sixty."

Folke raises his pelvis in his seat. His legs shoot out in the footwell of the passenger side, up rises his crotch, and then one hand works its way with difficulty into his sweatpants. While Sonja's defying death in the right lane, Folke rummages around for something down in his sweats. It's hard to concentrate, but then Folke pulls out a pack of licorice lozenges.

"Give me your hand," he says.

Sonja's staring at the rusty back doors of a white van.

"Out with your paw, Sonja," says Folke.

She sticks out her paw.

"You're doing great," he says, and then she feels the lozenge on her palm at the same time that Folke flips on the stereo.

It's Rammstein on CD. Not that Sonja can tell the difference between Rammstein and so much else, but then Folke asks her if she doesn't love Rammstein, and what's she supposed to say? Sonja's into classical music, she's into jazz and American troubadours, and there are vehicles in many lanes. Rammstein and Folke sing in unison, and the cars whizz like arrows through the morning. Cars of every color on their way south, and she's driving through the gateway to Denmark. *The road home*, Sonja thinks. *The road to Jutland, Europe, and Møns Klint. Oh, I'm scared.*

"I really don't know anything about music," Sonja lies, but there are too many big trucks and junctions, there's a licorice-chewing man riding shotgun, there are gummy bears and the speed encasing the car and all that insecurity, and then, with a lozenge in her mouth, Rammstein, sixth gear, *schnell, schnell*!

"Over there's a church for the deaf," Folke says, turning down the music a notch.

Sonja avoids looking in the direction Folke's pointing.

"I've often wondered how they run their services. I mean, I understand that the minister preaches in sign language. But what about when they're going to sing? How do you get a sanctuary full of deaf people to start the hymn at the same time?"

Sonja hangs behind the rusty van. In her rearview mirror, she can see the cab of an eighteen-wheeler. It looks like Ellen's cat, flat and evil in the face, and it's not good to be packed in like this. She has to get past the big vehicles. She shouldn't just sit there and let herself get squeezed.

"Does the minister stand down in front of them and shout, ONE, TWO, THREE, AND SING?"

Sonja's stopped breathing with her abdomen. Her breathing sits at the top of her ribcage. It's pistoning up and down, her fingers buzzing, her nose too. The eighteen-wheeler behind her is glossy and green. The van in front of her looks as if it's ready to have its plates confiscated. She herself is hyperventilating. She could get into a situation that she simply can't get out of. If the lane to the left closes off. If the trucks box her in. *I could find myself in a situation where the only way out is up*, thinks Sonja, but there's no escape route above the freeway. There's only a heavy August sky, and she's nauseous, and Folke's slid his sunglasses up on top of his head.

"You'd imagine that a church like that full of singing deaf people would sound like hell, but it's fascinating, and if you'd just glance back into your blind spot to the right you'll be fine. We're ready for the launch ramp."

Driving instructor lingo again. Sonja doesn't understand, and it's dangerous not to understand.

"We're going to look behind us," Folke says, and he looks behind them. "Signal, signal," he says, and he reaches across Sonja and sees to it that Sonja gets her right blinker on. "And now you can move to the right."

Sonja blindly enters the exit ramp that drops them into a suburb of Copenhagen. She doesn't know which suburb, and she doesn't know where she should go. She thought they were going to Køge, but now she feels like throwing up, if only it wouldn't make such a mess in the car. *A person can also be* too *mellow*, she thinks, and she looks carefully over at Folke. Being too mellow can be an expression of anxiety, she knows, and there sits Folke with his beard newly trimmed, phlegmatic and almost lazily slung against the side of the car. Is he stoned? she wonders. He might well be stoned.

"That went just fine," he says.

"I was scared of being boxed in."

"Aren't we all?" he says, and claps her on her gear hand.

"I don't think I'll ever learn to drive a car," she says, and now she can feel its onset again, the crying.

It sticks in her throat like a teasel. It's on the point of shooting up and out of her face. Her face is a sieve that would let water trickle right out, and she has to focus to shut it off. It must not happen, but that it very nearly does is all Folke's fault. Or is it also the fault of his small touchings, the lozenges in her palm, the scent of Magic Tree and is it suntan lotion?

"I've never had to give up on a student," Folke says. "And the students I did consider dropping were almost blind."

"I feel a bit blind too," says Sonja.

"Afraid," says Folke. "But that's only natural. You have to learn to be practical in the car."

"But I don't have any practical intelligence."

"You *are* intelligent, though. Just think about all the stuff you told me about the deer. That stuff with the exclosures, give me a break."

Sonja's eyes are burning, and it's good that they've turned onto a quiet road with abundant greenery on both sides. It almost looks like a piece of wilderness, but it isn't, it's Valby Park, and Folke wants to teach her to park here. They're also going to try backing around a corner. She could also just let the tears come, for she has the sense that Folke's seen a bit of everything in the car, but he compliments her for her parallel parking. He says that women are good at parking. He says that women listen too much to men who claim that women can't park. Women should stop listening to those kinds of men.

"The world's full of dickless men," says Folke.

But he shouldn't say dick *in the car*, thinks Sonja, backing tidily around a corner. Folke claps her on the gear hand. He says that she's driving just fine.

Yeah, I do it just fine backward, thinks Sonja. *I'm best in the wrong direction, and he shouldn't say* dick *in the car.*

"I miss nature in Copenhagen," she says aloud.

Folke points out at Valby Park.

"That's not nature," she says.

"If you keep going, on through Valby Park in the direction of South Harbor, you'll come to Tippen. Haven't you ever been to Tippen?"

"Don't know what it is."

"It's nature, Sonja, and that's all you're getting for your nickel today. Time's up."

They're suddenly done with practicing backing up. Now they're in traffic again, through Copenhagen and back to headquarters. It goes well, considering. Sonja thinks she can tell she's gotten better. She signals and twists her body in all the blind spots, mirror, shoulder, signal. The gears work, and it may be a game with Death, but it's all done and dusted for this time, the game, and Sonja reduces her speed to turn right. A couple of cyclists whip past, and then the road's clear. She turns into the narrow street to Folke's Driving School.

And then there are the steps, and who have we here?

We've got Jytte, solid as a tank. Jytte with her heart of gold and her disappointment. Jytte with her *kvørks*.

17.

SONJA FOLLOWS THE TRACK in through the firs. It's winter, she imagines. She's got hiking boots on so her socks won't get wet. The air is thick with moisture, the soil smells acidic. The needles droop dolefully on the firs, for darkness descends early in the day. Before it reaches the inland dunes the sun drops, and Sonja traipses onward. Her feet know the path they want to take. Sometimes it's best to let her boots sweep through the tough scrub; other times it's best to stand still. The stars are dim in the winter twilight, but visible, and the whooper swans have settled in for the winter by a small pond, farther out. She's brought the binoculars along, she imagines, and she's walking out to see the swans. She just has to follow the track in through the clearing, out onto the open heath, and then out past that. When she stands out on the heath, she can't see anything. Or she can see a lot, but there are no wires here, no brick transformer towers, no silos or deer stands. She's out beyond the reality of others, and the landscape's welcome to start moving. Sonja's been thinking of joining in. Now the swans are singing too. They float on their little pond and look so white in the twilight. They hymn and wheel in great arcs up across the landscape. Somewhere on the periphery, herds of deer are drifting in. She sits down on a tussock of grass and gazes down at her yellow clogs.

"And you could have fucking said you were too delicate to drive with me," Jytte says.

Whooper swans with white flight feathers, clogs with yellow snouts, Sonja's absence dissipating.

"How old exactly are we now? Couldn't manage to tell me yourself, had to get Folke to do it for you? Can't do anything on your own without getting Dad to jump in?"

The whooper swans gliding around on the water; the yellow clogs chafing carefully against each other.

"Know what we used to call someone like you in Djursland?"

"Chicken," says Sonja.

"Chicken *and* snitch," says Jytte.

She's lit another cigarette, her gaze rheumy, while Sonja's over forty and in two places at once. She's standing on a side street in a capital city that won't have anything to do with her, yet she's also far away in the landscape. She's grown up and playing the part, but she's also a child who doesn't want to learn her lesson, who won't adapt, won't be like the others and think what the others think, whatever that might be. She wants to get free, utterly free, and so she has to take flight, and it's as if, the moment she saw Jytte approaching, Sonja pressed an elevator button in her mind. The doors opened, then Sonja stepped in and departed skyward. While Jytte was grinding out her first butt under her shoe, Sonja disappeared from the picture unnoticed. Up and away with her, into the unknown like in that film *Contact* with Jodie Foster, where Jodie whooshes through the universe's wormholes all alone. She's shaking in the driver's seat of the spaceship, takes off her seatbelt, floats around the capsule and screams in terror until everything goes quiet and she's staring at a distant galaxy "no words can describe," she says. "They should have sent a poet," Jodie says, and then she's mentally transported to a memory: a Florida beach with the swash of waves and her dead father calmly plodding over to the beleaguered actress. "I missed you," her father says. "I'm sorry I couldn't be there for you, sweetheart," and then they stand there speaking intimately, the alien disguised as her father, and Jodie Foster disguised as Sonja. "You feel so lost, so cut off, so alone," her father says, and what he's talking about is humanity's sense of isolation in the universe, and Jodie asks, "What happens now?" And her father, who's also an alien, says, "Now you go home," and Sonja whizzes through the universe in a bubble of sheet metal and aluminum back to the sidewalk, where Folke has left her to stand alone and make a spectacle of herself with the goddess of vengeance.

"I've actually never seen the like," says Jytte. "But now you can content yourself with Folke and see how you like them apples. Just don't expect to come crawling back to me. That is, if you're even capable of learning to drive. It's not like it was very easy driving around with *you*."

Sonja's sinking down. Now she lands on both legs. They're long, and there's something storky about them. Atop the legs, the pelvis sits a touch askew. The hip sockets, the spine, and the neck, which she's holding rigid. At the pinnacle is the short hair in a pleasant do, but the do doesn't diminish the blows that Jytte dishes out. And the mouth with its queer shape cannot get said what it ought to. *And it's ugly to boot*, Sonja thinks, for Jytte's fury strikes inward, and Sonja has to fumble with her bag. Inside there's a chapstick, a phone and a bottle of water.

"I don't think there's any way I can learn to drive," Sonja whispers.

"Then you should maybe consider saving your pennies," says Jytte.

"But I'd like to be allowed to make the attempt," says Sonja. "That's all."

"And what, I didn't let you?" asks Jytte, for she's grown up among farmers and knows the drill with muzzles, with pee, with dogs and driving students who are a little too old. *Jytte's living proof*, Sonja thinks, *of how far you can move without getting anywhere*, and she looks at the door to Folke's Driving School. Folke's sitting somewhere inside, having abandoned her to this.

"No, you didn't really let me do the driving myself," says Sonja. "*How am I supposed to learn?* I thought, and so . . ."

She risks a glance down at Jytte. She's about the same height as Kate and Paul, because he was pretty short too. That meant he could stand there and look at her young-girl's breasts, for they never did get any larger, which was something that no doubt attracted him, while she stood there and regarded his expanding bald spot. *And from this altitude*, thinks Sonja, *you shouldn't reckon on anything but disappointment.* Jytte's no exception. Her livid face. The smoker's wrinkles. The gold earrings dragging her earlobes down to her shoulder pads. The whole package looks exactly like what it is: a bingo night wreck. *And yet in the end*, thinks Sonja, *no*—for once Jytte was sitting in a Djursland kitchen that was much too large. She'd been eating her brown-sugar sandwich. She was waiting for the bell to ring, for life to get rolling with its escape attempts, its broad boulevards, its lunches with men in uniform. That had been the sort of thing that wagged its tail in Jytte's dreams, and to get what she wanted, she had to act the part she thought would fit the theater piece.

Now the role hangs on Jytte like old rags.

"You didn't really let me do the driving myself," Sonja says again. "I wasn't allowed to take any responsibility in the car."

Jytte's mouth grows white and pursed.

"You know, don't you, that Folke snagged his last wife while teaching her to drive?"

Sonja didn't know, but there's something to the picture.

"No skin off *my* nose," says Sonja.

"Says you!"

Says me, thinks Sonja, and she turns on her heel, yes, she turns her back on Jytte and sets a course up the street. She walks away from the confrontation without saying goodbye. Not saying goodbye isn't something Sonja learned at home. In Balling, you always said a polite farewell, but Sonja feels she's got a right to leave the scene of the crime. *You're allowed to flee the blows you're being dealt*, thinks Sonja, and someplace high above the scene, in the skies above San Diego, Ellen would nod approvingly if she had the slightest clue.

Small insurrections count too, Sonja says to herself as she walks around Frederiksberg, unseeing. *Small refusals and choices can make the difference between life and death. If Jodie hadn't entered that bar with the pinball machine; if Jodie hadn't taken her seatbelt off in the spaceship. It's the small margins that decide the outcome, and there's got to be struggle if your life's going to grow, and your life* should *grow*, thinks Sonja, *though ideally not inward. On the other hand, it's dangerous to become addicted to your life's little dramas. The city's full of drama junkies, and I'm not one of them. I'm satiated*, she thinks, and she turns up Gammel Kongevej at high speed. Her legs feel wobbly, but the local city hall is a short distance ahead, and back behind the city hall lies Frederiksberg Gardens, with all its hiding places and benches. She wants to walk back in there and over to a bench. She hurries up the street and then crosses at the big intersection by Falkoner Boulevard, and then it's on into the park. Long strides past the lawn of bulbs that have long since withered, long strides down the path past the Chinese Pavilion, and then she cuts her speed. Her legs don't want to move so fast anymore, or else it's just Sonja who doesn't, because adrenaline functions fine as long as you have to survive. It's only later that you pay the piper.

She sits down on a bench with a view of the herons' little island. The herons roost on the guano-bespattered branches like spindly candleholders on a Christmas tree. It looks as if they could tumble down at any moment and set fire to the entire thing. Their throats are noisy too, when they're not standing still in the water with their fixed stares. In flight, they resemble vultures on the lookout for a corpse, but when they stand still in the water, they look more like the man with the scythe.

Now I'm here, thinks Sonja, *and it's just birds—somewhat tame birds, but birds.*

Sonja feels ashamed, yet also quite satisfied. In Balling, you certainly learned never to oppose a teacher. No, you weren't ever supposed to oppose anyone who'd shinnied up the pecking order, though it wasn't as if Dad held himself back. One minute the two of them would be tiptoeing into the grain, hunting down wild oats. The next, Dad would be walking around down by the property line, scattering foxglove seed. He made sure to throw some across the line, onto the property of Marie's father. Marie's father hated anything that wasn't useful to agriculture, and foxglove had absolutely no utility. Dad's sweetbriars, dog roses, jewelweeds and other such folderol were a thorn in the eye of any real farmer. But Dad scattered foxglove seed across the line. He sowed poppies, cornflowers and other trumpery. Then he waited till the next summer, when Marie's father would be standing down by the transformer tower, froth at the corners of his mouth. He would stand there in a sea of flowers, and Sonja's father loved the sight of flowers, while Sonja loved the sight of her father. His warm smile, her small supporting role as daughter, and when harvest approached he'd send her out into the barley. She was supposed to hunt down the wild oats, and Sonja would slither happily through the surface of the grain and point the weeds out to Dad. One two three *snap!* and afterward the scrap of love from Dad's palm when she called herself *field mouse.*

But that was eons ago, thinks Sonja, *and there's not much of that I can claim to have harvested, the love of men that is, and now here we are. In Frederiksberg Gardens, with filthy birds and happy people, and I'm not one of them. No, I'm not one of them.*

18.

THERE ARE THREE THINGS on Sonja's desk. The Gösta manuscript, the connective-tissue letter to Kate, and Sonja's lease. She pulled out the last item just after she came back from her driving lesson. No, correction: she pulled it out just after she walked into the bedroom and shoved her double bed over into the corner. She'd found herself by the door to the bedroom, her jaw muscles aching, and there stood the bed, ostentatiously placed in the middle of the floor so that Sonja and a given lover could approach it from either side. *A waste of floor space*, she thought, and it was simply a question of voting against its placement with the balls of her feet and pushing it into a corner. Into the corner with it. Single-side access should suffice.

Now she sits at the desk and considers the manuscript. No matter what Sonja does with her life, she's sure that Gösta will be just fine. He won't even miss her. Right behind Sonja stands the next person who can fill the role of Gösta's voice in Danish, so if she ignored the financial void, she could easily choose to be free. Sonja's dispensable, hardly a beneficial species, and next to it's the letter to Kate. Sonja's peeled the stamps off because it's better to use them for letters that will actually be sent. She's opened the envelope too, and it's a good thing she didn't send it, the gum was sticking so poorly. The letter might have slipped out at a postal facility, fallen into the hands of some sorting machine operator, and ended up on a staff room bulletin board as an example of family friction.

I'm angry, thinks Sonja. *I'm angry but mustn't show it. If I show it, I'll lose Kate, and Frank will follow, their kids too, and someday Mom and Dad will die, and if I look to my future, I can't remember jack, but now in any case I'm done with yearning for the big prize, and still I must not get angry.* Anger brings loneliness, and then they'd sit and giggle about it at the West Jutland Sorting Facility while Kate never got the letter.

No, Kate'll never get the letter, because Sonja has slid it out of the envelope. She's reread it and determined that it actually doesn't say anything worth mentioning. A bit about Bacon Bjarne, *and good riddance to him. Good riddance to all of it*, Sonja thinks, and she looks at the lease. It's with the apartment co-op that Sonja by some miracle became a member of, back in the day. In fact it's been very practical. Living conditions have been orderly, without any direct contact with the landlord. But the stiff owls on the other balconies haunt her every time she looks out of the window. It should really be barnacle geese or other migratory fowl. Not pigeons and plastic owls and herons. Whooper swans! Bitterns! Graylags and other living creatures that cross the sky in magnificent V-formations. Yearning, buoyancy.

As if Sonja's conjured it, a helicopter drifts by above the backyard, stoic in gray metal. While she sits there following it with her gaze, she can barely recall what it was that brought her to Copenhagen. It was her friendship with Molly, yes, and the longing to make something out of her complications. To take what was dragging her down in the one place and transform it into something that raised her up in the other. It was a choice—for what would have become of her in Balling? For an entire year of primary school, the girls in her class dreamed of becoming dog groomers, but how many dog groomers was there room for in western Jutland, their teacher asked, and most of the girls ended up working in nursery schools or home care. What would Sonja have done with the local kids? She who thought there was more to life. Something bigger, perhaps. *I can always have kids later*, Sonja said, and Mom said as much too, but it was just a way to say that Sonja didn't really want kids. In Copenhagen you could have something else, and her first years there were a success. She learned the city's movements, its dialog, its form. But bit by bit it stopped making sense.

Her jaw's tensing up again, and she gets up from the desk. She finds her phone and lies down on the bed. It works just fine, crawling in from one side, and then she makes a call. She wants to grasp at something in the other direction: backward. There's nothing in Copenhagen but people who are like people of every shape and size anywhere. Nothing more, nothing less, just people, and besides, they rarely meet anyone outside their segment anyway. They're like the big landholders who show up at a national congress and only want to hang out with each other, they reek of Old Spice, they have the same opinions, the same interests, and when they want to stick out from the crowd they stick out in the same way. In the Jutlandic hinterlands, it's 4x4s and gleaming herbicide sprayers; in Copenhagen, it's Christiania cargo bikes, bushy beards, and lockstep diversity. Everything she'd thought she'd grow into turned out to be just as fallibly human as what Molly thought they were getting away from. But the place you come from is a place you can never return to. *It no longer exists*, Sonja thinks, trying to swallow the lump in her throat, *and you yourself have become a stranger.*

It's Mom and Dad she's calling. It's been a long time since she last spoke to them. The phone rings in Jutland, but it rings in vain. Mom's probably out in the yard, and Dad often takes out his ears. Then he stands and converses loudly with a neighbor, while his hearing aids lie on the kitchen counter and whine, *but as long as they're both well*, thinks Sonja, hanging up as yet another helicopter approaches. And another. It's an entire swarm. *They must be conducting exercises*, thinks Sonja, *or else the anarchists have regrouped. Maybe they're milling around at the end of some street, throwing cobblestones. Could be terrorism too*, she thinks, and sits up halfway. The choppers are circling over something, it could be Vesterbro, and Sonja's getting agitated. Then she calls Kate. It happens of its own accord, instinctive, spontaneous. *There should have been barnacle geese!* she thinks. *Curlews! Fence posts!* She ought to drop out, slip into the stillness and then just lie there, watching for sparrow hawks over by the firs. *I've done my service! I've learned my lesson!*

There's a soft beep in her ear each time the phone rings in Jutland. It rings again and again without going over to the answering machine. Now Kate's standing somewhere exposed, staring at the screen. She's standing and thinking so hard her head creaks. Poor excuses don't make themselves, and there's a limit to how many times you can claim you've run out of battery.

"Hello?" sounds suddenly from the other end of the line.

To Sonja it's a kick in the gut.

"Is that you, Kate?" she asks.

"Yes?" Kate's saying, and it sounds like she's fumbling with something. "Sonja, is that you? I hope nothing's wrong . . ."

"It *is* me, and why would anything be wrong? Nothing's wrong, I was just thinking I'd call and hear how things are going over there with you guys."

"They're going fine here," says Kate. "But you know what, I'm in the garden center now."

Sonja glances up at her small corner of late August sky. The window's open a crack, and she can hear the choppers swarming.

"Well good grief, over here the storm clouds are piling up. Have you been having a lot of thunderstorms there too?"

She's able to gather from Kate that it hasn't been so bad, but Sonja can tell her that here on the thickly peopled side of Denmark, a violent storm is raging.

"Probably from some of that climate stuff," she says, even though Kate once told her that she doesn't believe in that climate stuff because climate change is a question of faith, like joining the Jehovah's Witnesses, even though her husband travels the world over in the service of wind energy. That's how it is with so many things, and just to say *climate stuff* is to open a rift between the sisters Hansen.

"That doesn't sound so good," says Kate, "but I'm standing here in the garden center. We ran out of potting soil, so we can't—"

"Speaking of potting soil," Sonja hears herself say, "you know who crossed my mind the other day? Bjarne, weirdly enough—Bacon Bjarne. He wasn't particularly nice to you, back when you broke up with him, and I think it's strange that Dad sold the farm to him. There ought to really be some sort of limit to what a person is forced to swallow."

"Ohhh . . . I don't know about that now," says Kate. "He did have the money."

Sonja strains to catch the sound of other garden center customers in the background, but it sounds more like Kate's standing in her back passage at home. Out by the dryer.

"But he really wasn't very nice to you, Kate. He slapped you—but let's let bygones be bygones. You see anything of Tonny these days?"

"Not so much now. Tonny and Marie moved to Funen, you know."

"What's Marie doing with such a dope anyway?"

"Tonny's all right," says Kate, her voice taking on a note of forced cheeriness. "And we do miss Marie. She was the salad girl at our potlucks."

"He showed me his prick out by your dryer once, Tonny did, and it wasn't much to write home about, his prick that is, and you remember that kid from the special ed class who every so often would pull out his tool and walk around with it saying BANG BANG down by the bike shed? And then men go claiming there isn't any connection between their dicks and New Year's fireworks, to say nothing of the rifle club in Balling. I imagine they're looking forward to neutralizing some stags when the season starts. Dad says the herds are getting more and more unruly."

It's quiet on the other end of the line. Not even the slightest rustle from a bag of soil being lowered into a shopping cart.

"But who gives a rat's ass about that?" asks Sonja. "As long as Marie's doing well. It can't be that easy, with her Indre Mission background, to have Tonny in tow. Or maybe it's the Mission background that compels Tonny to go around airing his tulip. One time we were supposed to bring in urine samples for the school nurse, and Marie forgot her pee, and in retrospect it may well have been that in spite of all the hogs her dad had in the barn, they didn't deal with pee at all in the Mission. At least not girl pee."

Now Kate sighs.

"Tell you what, Sonja—Frank's traveling, so why don't we chat another day? The boys are coming home for the weekend and we're going to have pork roast, so I also need to stop by the supermarket."

"Pork rift?"

"Pork roast!"

Sonja sits down so she has a better view of the sky. It's a good thing she moved the bed, because now she's able to see upward, and there's still a buzz of helicopters, and she tells Kate that she once had her fortune told by a fortune teller. It's Sonja's impression that at this point in their relationship, she can tell Kate whatever she wants to, assuming her sister answers the phone, because Kate sidesteps everything. Just so there are no speed bumps in the conversation, and while Sonja does miss her sister, at the same time it ignites a yearning in her for fire. She wants to flush Kate from the bushes. Kate needs to show herself, she needs to speak plainly and wield the sort of arms, legs, and persona that would want to embrace her neighbor.

"Yeah, I went to this party at Molly's, you see, and there was this fortune teller who I didn't manage to stop in time.

She interpreted my future, and I've forgotten most of it, but as far as I can recall she was quite detailed. You remember that German translator? Paul? Well anyway, she said something about him, and the weirdest thing about it is that I can't remember the rest of it now. In a sense I lost my future because she told me about it. That's been bugging me lately, and it's not going so great with the driver's license either. I think my driving instructor has designs on me. He probably thinks I'm desperate, and I am, but not in that—"

"Did she say anything about me?" interrupts Kate.

"Who?" asks Sonja, and Kate is *not* walking around a garden center.

That sound in the background is a golden retriever scratching on a door, and Sonja's not so unhousebroken that she can't recognize the sound of a washing machine announcing that it's finished.

"You want to know if the fortune teller said something about you?"

"Yes," says Kate hesitantly. "It could be quite amusing to know. Since I had my knee operated, it hasn't been working properly."

"That doesn't sound so good," Sonja whispers.

"And we've got this new neighbor. Some divorced man or other from Aalborg, and he's got a job out with Frank. Such a loner. I haven't talked to him, but he walks around over in his yard, setting mole traps and glaring over the hedge."

"I don't think she said anything about you," Sonja whispers. "I can't remember what she said, but I'm sure your neighbor's not a violent criminal."

"One never really knows," says Kate.

Sonja watches the rotors reflecting in the sunlight, and then she lies down.

"Are Mom and Dad doing okay?"

"They're fine, and now I'm by the cashier, so is it all right if we . . . ?"

Kate is standing by the cashier in her imaginary garden center. She lies expertly about the vegetation around her and says it was good to hear from Sonja, and Sonja says it was good to hear Kate's voice, and afterward, when they've hung up, Sonja folds herself up on the bed. It's been ages since she's closed herself up this way, like a drying rack, but at the moment it's the only thing that can provide comfort. The only acute medicine, and in the distance there's buzzing. Somewhere in Copenhagen the helicopters have risen with a purpose, and Sonja wishes she were hovering up there with them. Not so much in the middle of her life as with a view of it.

19.

THE BEST THING IN THE WORLD was to be taken up on her lap. To be lifted up and pressed into Mom's turtleneck. Mom's breasts under the fabric, the smell of her throat, the shiny picture cards in Sonja's fingers; the confidence that all would turn out well. Next best was the weight of Dad's hand on her head when she'd made him laugh. Gotten him to look at her as if she came from another planet. After these came playing with the others, but even better was playing by herself. Freedom resided in unpeopled spaces, in the bottom of closets, and as far back as she could go inside the chicken coop. A trail led out to it. And into it.

Once I hid during gymnastics, Sonja recalls, *back behind the equipment. I sat there under the vaulting horse and sniffed the leather and the untold generations of sweat. I remembered how Dad had fallen in love with Mom because she'd shone like a kingfisher in Skjern. The others were playing pirate tag in the gym, but under the horse, I sat with my knees up by my nose. I suppose I was painfully aware of my isolation and at the same time, hopelessly enamored with its possibility.*

It's green around her, green and warm, almost stifling, and she glances at the path in front of her. She walks as quickly as she can. She's trying to keep up.

The spirit of the times demands one thing of us, thinks Sonja. *Other people demand a second thing, and we ourselves something entirely different. If you're not careful, you stop getting it all to fit together, and then suddenly you're a helpless piece of meat trying to catch up to your driving instructor.*

Sonja looks up thc path. There's Folke's little ass, bobbing away from her a bit farther ahead. He zigzags in and out of the rosebushes, while his slender guitar fingers point out what she assumes are a product of the local fauna.

There's a mound, and there's another.

Folke's pointing at features that look like barrows, overgrown with grass, and Sonja's been following him while he's on the prowl for these great piles of earth, just as she'd once been on the prowl for wild oats.

Sonja did the driving on the way here, and it went pretty well. As long as they stay away from Vesterbro, she's amenable to instruction. With Jytte, Sonja was able to manage Istedgade by closing her eyes, but she hasn't been that deep into the heart of Copenhagen with Folke yet. Today they drove out of the city, and she knew already when she slid into the driver's seat that something was afoot.

He just handed her the keys, first gear, look back, flash flash with the blinker, and then they were off. He was a tad timid too, his arms crossed, and then that smell in the car.

Sunscreen?

It isn't Sonja's job to have an opinion on where the car's going. It's Folke who's got the map in his head, and it's Sonja's lot to be subject to his will. He can lead her wherever he wishes. She doesn't orient herself geographically at all, as she's busy with the gears and the practicalities of the car. "Throw the car, throw the car," he'll say, and then she'll pretend she has physical contact with it. She doesn't really, but when he says "right" she turns right, "left" left. Folke is Sonja's lord, he shall not want, and at one point out along Gammel Køge Landevej, he told her to execute a simple left-hand turn at some unexceptional intersection. Before she knew it they were out in the open. She thought it was because she was supposed to demonstrate once again that she's best when she's driving backward, but when they reached the end of a network of gravel roads riddled with unmarked intersections, Folke told her to park on what looked like a lawn.

"And now we're getting out of the car," he said, taking the keys out of the ignition and clenching them in his fist.

She had no desire to leave the Batmobile's interior. There was hardly a cell in her body that did not feel disinclined, but at some point she did have to learn how to put wiper fluid in the car. Something to do with the hood.

"If it's the hood, then I don't—"

"We're going this way," Folke had said, and off they went, because in this relationship he's the one who's directionally equipped. What does Sonja know about driving instructor pedagogy, other than that the student must relinquish her free will? Folke went first, then Sonja. In through a thicket of rugosa roses, down a trail by the water. Over past a windsurfing club and then beyond, beyond, with Folke's long legs a stride ahead the entire time.

Am I paying for this? Sonja wondered, instead of enjoying the prospect of the Avedøre power plant. Isn't this precisely the sort of thing I should refuse to pay a single crown for?

she asked herself, and then Folke opened a gate of the type that keeps in sheep.

"After you," he said, for she had finally halted.

"I really don't know . . ."

"I just want to show you Tippen," he said, hitching up his sweatpants in that way she doesn't care for, but in his face, in his eyes, Folke looked like a kid, so now they're walking, Sonja behind and Folke's little ass ahead, and he's pointing out piles of earth.

"There's one, and there's one more. You see 'em?"

The hillocks stick up out of a flat, grass-covered plain. It's pretty enough, Sonja can see that, but she'd have preferred to be here alone. In the early summer there must have been lots of elderflowers, and the roses are faded now, but Sonja can see the bushes flourishing hither and yon—rugosa roses, sweetbriar roses, dog roses—roses aplenty. In among them, the trunks of birches poke up pale and proud, though a garden tractor has gashed a track through the wilderness.

It doesn't count then, thinks Sonja. *That's definitely cheating.*

"There's one more, and there's another. Exciting, huh?"

It's the strategically laid-out mounds that Folke wants her to notice, and then they're almost down by the water. In the distance, Avedøre Power Station towers like an intergalactic castle. Somewhere over to the left, Amager Nature Reserve stretches out toward the airport, planes are aloft, and a freeway bridge spans the horizon, though she can hardly hear any traffic. *They should have sent a poet*, thinks Sonja.

"Gorgeous, eh?" says Folke.

"Yeah, some nice mounds," says Sonja.

"They're scrapheaps. Garbage!" cries Folke, and he puts a hand to his beard. "Garbage, ha!"

They've turned so that they're standing with the water on one side and a large mound on the other, and it's this mound that Folke dips his head toward now.

"That's the remains of the Gestapo headquarters downtown, the Shell House. They didn't know where else to cart the shit, and so someone came up with the idea of just hauling it out to the dump at South Harbor. It's hard to see it now, but you have to imagine that in the forties, this here was a scrapyard. A rubbish tip, Sonja. A war zone. German trucks, the Gestapo, Danish forced labor, just picture it."

Folke rotates, his arms extended.

"It was an incredible Allied action," he says. "The Germans had stuck the resistance fighters out of the way just under the roof of Shell House. They were sitting up there twiddling their thumbs like human shields, but the Allies knew that, so they flew in from the side, BOOM. It wasn't just that they got the Nazi swine on the lower floors, because they did, but lots of the resistance folk were lucky enough to escape."

"They also hit a Catholic school in Frederiksberg."

"You know the story?" Folke asks, astonished, and he walks over toward the scrapheap.

"A bit," says Sonja, and then Folke and his long legs start clambering around in the scrap.

He shows her the tender shoots of elder and birch. He shoves small cement blocks to the side, and he holds up pieces of building debris so that she can see it better.

One morning long ago, thinks Sonja, *some trash hauler wrestled all this crap up onto the bed of a truck with bad suspension. He shoveled*

Shell House up off the street, corpse stench and all, and then he drove it out here. He gazed over at the Amager reserve and shoveled all the misery into a pile. The human capacity for moving on is unique, thinks Sonja. *Our adaptability's remarkable. Except for mine. Mine limps behind*, she thinks, looking out across the lacerated landscape, which is not a landscape but a garbage dump that's been allowed to grow afterward.

If the panoramic experience of nature can be compared to drugs, then this is a wad of used nicotine gum, thinks Sonja. *But people like Folke fled the countryside generations ago. What do they know?*

"It's lovely here," says Sonja. "You come out here often?"

"I was born over there," says Folke, pointing in the direction of outer Vesterbro. "So we'd come over here to play and make forts and kiss girls."

Something gives in Sonja, and she starts walking. She walks down to the water. There's a path down there, and she bears right. It might be the way they came, she can't remember, for this is not her territory, and she has no clue how they came down here or how she'll get back to the vehicle. It's Folke who decides, and he's also the one with the keys. Some distance out in the water, a sail sweeps past, and then another. It's the windsurfers, and it's good to have humans nearby. *Potential witnesses*, thinks Sonja, who can hear Folke hurrying along behind her.

"Easy, easy!" Folke calls out, catching up with her. "What's up with you? The car's back up there."

Now he's pointing again, but in the opposite direction, and Sonja's jaw tenses. He starts to grasp her upper arm but she isn't having any of it, she snatches her arm from his grip.

"Glad to hear it!" she yells, while the waves slosh the old tires, the used condoms, the cola bottles around. "Why the hell can't I just learn to drive?"

Folke takes two steps back. He does this demonstratively, with his hands raised a bit in the air, a bit like John Wayne when someone's finally caught him at close range in some town far out on the prairie. The locals have hidden in the saloon, the brothel, in the trees and scrub, but now Sonja's calling him out on a trash trail in South Harbor.

"I just want to learn how to drive, okay? I don't want to have my hand held, I don't want to be massaged, hugged or interrogated, to be hit on or coochie-cooed. I want to learn to drive that car so I can drive over there!"

Sonja can point too, and what she points at is Avedøre Power Station, but also behind it, at Denmark and the world in general.

"I want an ordinary Class B driver's license, and all the other bullshit you people dish up is stuff I got wise to a long time ago. I'm over forty, and I've learned it the hard way, so don't push your Gestapo on me."

Folke lowers his arms and walks carefully over to the little bank that slopes down to the shore. Then he sits down on the edge and smacks his hands against his kneecaps. His beard curls down toward his driving instructor's belly, but the top of his head is ruddy and bare, and now he raises up a bit, up with the crotch. He works a hand down in his pocket, and up comes a little tin. Folke gets the tin open, and a finger deep into it. On the tip of his finger, Sonja can see a cream-like substance, and it's going onto Folke's head. Now he's smearing his bare scalp in cream. Now he's sitting and looking out over the water. A black windsurfer sail crosses in toward him from the one side, a gull flutters past from the other, and there are coots too. Seen with his back to her, Folke looks like someone who's had his ears boxed. A male ego in retreat, fragile and easily bruised, someone to treat with kid gloves, yet at the same time human too. And Sonja will be damned if that trick doesn't work every time. *If a man just has to seem like a human being*, she thinks.

"It wasn't meant in that way, you know," Sonja says. "You're an excellent teacher, it's not that."

"It's no damn picnic going to work and then being yelled at like that."

Foot doctor problems, thinks Sonja, but she knows that ploy and it doesn't interest her, she doesn't want to go there, and her silence prompts Folke to embellish his alibi.

"It's not so often I drive with someone my own age," he says. "Those eighteen-year-olds are nice enough, but they're *kids*, and they're into some crazy shit."

"The future, for instance," Sonja suggests.

"More like tattoos and shit like that," says Folke.

Sonja sits down on the bank at a safe distance; she doesn't want him to get confused, but to judge by his face, he isn't. He's embarrassed, his lower lip protruding like Dad's would when Mom rebuked him. When his boyish nature received a rap on the knuckles, Dad would wallow in misgiving, and then it wouldn't be long before Mom would indicate the gun cabinet and suggest he go out into the farthest part to shoot partridge and hare.

It was all about reestablishing the sensation in his cock, Sonja thinks, and Mom knew that. By and large, that was something that women learn with time: how much psychology resides between men's legs, and if you can be bothered, you learn to deal with it, and if you can't, then you sit here with your driving instructor looking out across the water toward Hvidovre Harbor.

"Well, here we are," says Folke. "Sitting in the middle of nature and catching our breath."

"This isn't nature," says Sonja. "Back where I come from, we've got a heath so large and ancient that it's developed its own consciousness."

"It probably has," says Folke. "All the Jutlanders I've met are a bit quirky, and I'm going to teach you how to drive. Don't you worry your head about it," he says, and then he laughs a bit goofily.

Sitting there, with his long legs and cloven hooves hanging over the bank, *all he needs is a pair of antlers to appear a little stately*, Sonja thinks. A handsome man, in theory, but other women's men are a closed chapter, and now I want to go home. Yes, I want to go home.

She feels the way a toddler must feel when it rocks back on its heels and stands still. I want to go home, she repeats to herself, and that's pretty good: she's a toddler, and she's standing still. Afraid that the feeling will evaporate, she stops picking at it. She shelves it and squints down at her feet. They're encased in sensible driving shoes, and they dangle undisturbed far beneath her. She knocks them lightly against each other; they seem to suit her.

"This hour's a freebie," says Folke. "I just wanted to show you how the grass has grown over everything here. That you no longer can tell it was a war zone, can you?"

There's a buzzing behind them, an angry sound rising from the grass back in Tippen. From the bushes step a couple of young guys with long limbs. One's got a joystick in his hand, and both their faces are turned skyward. They're flying a miniature remote-controlled thingamajig. The thingamajig sounds like a riled-up mosquito, but its form is more that of a dragonfly, a large gleaming one. The electronic dragonfly loops in broad figure eights above the boys and swerves out over Folke and Sonja as they sit there, dangling their legs over the edge of what once was Shell House.

20.

There was a period when Sonja wanted to learn the recorder. She wanted to do it on her own, though, it had to happen alone. She would have nothing to do with instruction; she refused. She could walk out into the rye, or it could also be in the farthest part. But out there there were whooper swans, and sometimes there were hunters in the area. They had long rifles and didn't care for nature lovers who roamed about and startled the game. But it could also be in one of the jagged windbreaks. She loved watching them as she sat in the backseat of Dad's car en route from one place to another. There was something about the way the trees materialized against the sky—especially when there was rime on the needles. But the curious thing was that though she loved *looking* at windbreaks, she didn't like to *be* in them.

Marie and Sonja had once made a fort in the windbreak along the property line. They were going to have bug juice, crackers, and secret exercise books there. But it was a lame fort, and Marie wasn't much help at making it cozy. The rough Sitka spruce tore holes in their clothes, and the floor of the windbreak was barren and littered with needles. Sitka needles were lovely from a distance, but close up they pricked you cruelly. When the two girls sat there being secret in their exercise books, Sonja would write about homesickness and pain, and it was the windbreak's fault. Windbreaks were practical for farming, and they had a certain visual effect, but they were lifeless inside, and Sonja didn't want to play the recorder there. It was out of the question.

But behind the myrobalan plums and the other fruiting bushes in Mom's garden, there hid a bird cherry. The tree had grown huge and reminded you of nothing so much as an enormous shrub. If you plucked the flowers and brought them into the house, they stank of cat piss, but outdoors the scent was almost delightful. Sonja got ahold of an old lawn chair. Your butt would slip through the seat if you sat in it, so Mom had let her have it. With persistence, Sonja had succeeded in dragging the chair partway up the bird cherry. She wedged the chair legs down in a couple of forks of the tree, and then she would sit there in the middle of the branches. When she blew on the recorder, she sounded like a blackbird. That's what she imagined; that people walking by on the gravel road would take her for a bird. And when the wind blew through the crown, the green bottles she'd hung from one of the branches sang along. They sounded like a bittern out in the reeds, and the bittern out in the reeds sounded like a ship that hooted in the fog, and the sound drew Sonja to other realms.

Even though Kate knew perfectly well where Sonja was hiding, she left her in peace. Besides, she'd once had an animal cemetery under the bird cherry. When Sonja peered down through the branches, she could still see Kate's cemetery down there. Small crosses bound neatly together with wire, the plots laid with gravel fetched from the farmyard. It was all washing away now, because then Kate had been confirmed, and her head only had room for boys and pop music. It was strange how she'd changed, for at one point, Kate had been so desperate to find animals to inter that she buried a live earthworm. But that came to an end, and once it did, Sonja would sit up on a branch where no one could reach her. She'd peer up at the sky through the tangle of limbs. Every so often, she'd carve away at the trunk a bit with a dull breadknife from the kitchen drawer. Then it would smell sourly of sap.

One day she pretended that she had visions in the tree. That the light filtered down through the crown and fluttered about her face in such a way that it might well have been an angel. The angel wanted everything good to happen to Sonja, and it specifically told Sonja how good her life would become. It caressed her cheek. That's how Sonja imagined it—the angel fondling her the way she fondled their kitten. She let herself be petted until Kate called her to come and eat. They were having red wieners with potatoes and white sauce, Kate shouted, for she always stuck to the pull of gravity like that, and Sonja wishes she were sitting in the bird cherry right now. Far up in the tree with her face tilted to the sky, but she's not. She's sitting next to Molly in a subway carriage. They're deep in the bowels of the earth, and they're on their way to the Danmarks Radio concert hall.

"Great that you could take time off on such short notice," says Molly.

"Gösta's not going anywhere," says Sonja.

Molly's been given free tickets to Brahms's Piano Concerto No. 1 by a client, and she's also had her hair done. Her heart-shaped face is glowing, and there's something electric about her. Sonja's familiar with this state of Molly's. She's seen it before. It's infatuation, and it can hardly be the lawyer who's inspiring it. *She looks like a child*, Sonja thinks, and yet there's something about her face, something closed off, that Sonja can't get a handle on. A hardening, which might originate from within Molly herself, but which could also very well stem from without. From injections. Molly wouldn't tell her if that were the case. To do that would be to expose herself, for Sonja's not the type to believe in the body as cosmetic project. For her own part, Sonja doesn't imagine telling Molly about the hike with Folke. It's the one thing Sonja promised herself before she left home: to never tell Molly about the outing to Tippen. For Molly, tales without a climax don't have any appeal.

"Tell me a little about what we're going to hear," says Molly. "I don't have a clue about classical music."

It's true. When Sonja's ridden in Molly's car, they've listened to Top 40 all the way to the house in Hørsholm. Yet Molly does play popular classical works—"Elvira Madigan," Carl Nielsen, the *Moonlight Sonata*—in her clinic waiting room. Day in, day out, the same pieces, deviously designed to create trust between an apprehensive client and psychologist Molly Schmidt, whom Sonja must confess she doesn't really know. No, Molly Schmidt hardly ever talks to Molly Pedersen of Skjern anymore, and Molly Pedersen never talks to Lone, which is Molly's real name, for the Molly business is something she came up with herself when she turned eighteen. "I'm a free individual," she'd said. "I can choose to be called whatever I want," she'd said, but on paper she's still Lone.

Sonja lets her eyes fall upon the far end of the train. It's clear that they're zipping through the subsoil without a driver like moles on speed. Kids are standing with their noses pressed flat against the panoramic front window, while an older woman is sitting a couple of seats up from Molly and Sonja. She's shriveled and short haired and doesn't look like she's from Copenhagen. In fact, she looks like a married woman from Jutland, with pleasant glasses and tidy hair. Her eyes are light blue, and she's keeping a firm grip on her handbag and her roll-along suitcase. *A country mouse*, thinks Sonja. She must have come over to see a family member who fled the provinces, doubtless a daughter.

"So tell me something about the music," Molly says.

Sonja wishes Molly had invited someone else to the concert, or that she'd been quicker on the trigger with an excuse, because now she's got to spend the entire journey from Nørreport to DR Byen acquainting Molly with the music.

"In Brahms's Piano Concerto No. 1, you should take special note of the adagio," Sonja begins.

Molly roots around in her bag, and the older woman farther up the car is rooting around in hers too. Sonja has a hard time holding the attention of her audience, but she soldiers on undaunted.

"Generally speaking, it seems to me that in classical music you should always keep an eye on the adagio, but in any case you *must* keep an eye on it in Brahms's piano concerto."

The gray woman takes a map of the city from her bag. She unfolds it neatly and holds it close to her face. Sonja doesn't feel she's being discreet enough about being from out of town. She'd like to tell the woman that it can be dangerous to advertise you're a tourist, but they'd gotten to the adagio, even though Molly's lost interest and is now busy texting someone.

"The adagio is the slow movement. The movement that's full of intimate emotion, tender and melancholy. Brahms was unhappily in love, and you can really hear it in his music. The interesting thing is that when Schumann's wife, Clara—for she was the one Brahms was hopelessly in love with—when Clara lost Schumann and Brahms was able to have her, he was no longer interested. He composed out of his painful distance from her. She was his muse, and of course there's nothing new in that, women as muses. The interesting thing is, I think that men function as muses for women just as often. Man as muse is an area of research that the Psychological Association should really challenge its members to study."

Molly says nothing. She's smiling absently at a text, and her smile smolders with things she wants to do but mustn't and then does anyway, for that's the kind of thing that makes the world go round.

It's not the lawyer, thinks Sonja, and a bit farther up in the passenger tribe, the gray woman sits with worry in her eyes. Her roll-along is squeezed between her legs, while the city map's up in her face. Beyond her, a couple of lanky pale hooligans are lounging idly about, the sort of kids who aren't going anywhere but just ride the train back and forth, back and forth. Molly's tapping away on her phone, the train's shooting through the underground, and then Sonja rises and takes a couple of steps up the aisle.

"Can you find where you're going?" asks Sonja, and the woman looks up.

Her face is wrinkled, but delicate and kind. Once her hair had been dark, but now it's silver. Her teeth are her own, though, and when she smiles they're clearly visible.

"I'm supposed to get out at Islands Brygge. My niece and her boyfriend have a flat there, but I'm not sure how to get from the station to where they live."

Sonja reaches for the map, and the train pulls into Kongens Nytorv. She asks the woman the name of the street, and the woman says it's called Jens Otto Krags Gade.

"That makes sense," says Sonja. "All the streets out there are named after dead prime ministers. She could also live on Erik Eriksen or Hans Hedtoft or someone even worse. The funny thing is that the same prime ministers are lying shoulder to shoulder out in Western Cemetery, stone cold dead. I'm rather fond of lying out there myself and reading. We don't do that in Jutland, but in Jutland there's plenty of room to lie down in places that aren't graveyards. Have you ever been to Western Cemetery?"

The woman hasn't.

"Your niece should take you. It's peaceful and quiet and quite lovely. Have you been traveling a long time?"

The woman has. She's been in transit most of the day, for there were technical problems in the Great Belt Tunnel, and Sonja asks her where she lives, and she lives in Vinkel, in western Jutland. She's lived there most of her life, so it's nothing special, and Sonja says small world, because she comes from Balling herself.

"You don't say!" says the woman, and a look of relief dawns in her face. "My sister and brother-in-law lived in Balling, but now she's dead. Her name was Esther, and his was Einar. Did you know them?"

Of course Sonja knows Esther and Einar—they were the ones who had the post office before it was closed down, and Sonja remembers their kids too, and now they've reached Christianshavn Station, and out of the corner of her eye, Sonja can see that Molly's flung herself in the corner of her seat. She slouches there with her phone up in her little face, tapping.

Maybe it's the shaman, thinks Sonja. Stranger things have happened in Molly's life, but it could also be a client. Even if Molly's not supposed to fuck them, but then there's so much you're not supposed to do, "And life is brief, so brief, and it could turn out / That you came too late to the end of your life," and Sonja has to admit that Molly's gradually become just like one of the windbreaks.

"What's your name?" Sonja asks.

The woman looks a little bashful, but she says her name's Martha.

"Martha?"

"Yes, there aren't so many of us with that name anymore. My parents belonged to Indre Mission. I don't, but one doesn't change one's name on that account."

"My name's Sonja. My parents were farmers and didn't know any better. Their taste in names was sort of like their taste in curtains. But one can be a good person all the same."

The woman grasps Sonja's arm by the elbow and gives it a small squeeze. She whispers that she's a tiny bit nervous. And tired. Copenhagen seems so big.

"It *is* big," Sonja says, and she glances at the woman's hand.

The hand has been accustomed to grabbing hold. It's been capable of shoveling everything from grain to muck and never complained, and then it hits Sonja that it's odd Martha's going to visit a niece. The gray ladies from Jutland usually visit their own kids and grandkids, but perhaps Martha has no kids; perhaps she's never been married. Though it didn't have a singles culture in any way, Balling did have plenty of single people. But they didn't raise a fuss about it, and to Sonja that seems right and fitting, for you'd have to look long and hard to find something more hideous than a singles culture. The hordes of people on maneuvers that are supposed to help auction them off like cattle, going in and out of restaurants with their heads full of dating services. Always alone, always between trysts, always headed somewhere else with sales narratives about who they think they should be in order to be a palatable version of themselves.

The old maids I knew as a child were good at gardening, thinks Sonja. *And good at reading, and folks enjoyed talking with them. They talked* about *them, sure, but they also talked* to *them, yes*, and just then the train pulls into Islands Brygge Station.

A quiet panic goes through Martha.

"Oh, it's here I get off, no?"

She's grabbed ahold of her heather-hued suitcase, and she doesn't want to let go of Sonja's arm, and that's all right. Sonja follows the woman over to the sliding door, and then they stand there faltering, especially Martha, who's trying to maintain decorum, to not stick out, to not look as if she doesn't have Copenhagen—which is chaos, just chaos—under control. She's crumpled the map around the handle of her roll-along, and Sonja thinks that Martha's niece could at least have met her at the station. But what does Sonja know about the kind of burden that the rest of the family thinks Martha might be? Nothing, and now the doors slide open. Molly looks over the top of her phone at Sonja. It seems as if she wants to say something, but she never gets round to it, because now Sonja's exited the carriage with Martha. She's off the train and on her way toward the stairs. It has to happen quick, for now Molly's risen in the middle of the passenger tribe. She stands with her small face turned toward the window, full of questions and caught between functions. She flutters the phone and her free hand. But Sonja's got no time to respond, and then Lone in the guise of Molly zooms under Amager while Sonja and Martha drift off toward the stairs. They're heading up to the light.

"I'll help you get over to Jens Otto Krag," says Sonja. "I'm going your way anyhow," she says.

"I thought you were going to hear Brahms," says Martha.

"No no, that was that other woman," Sonja lies, and she offers to take Martha's suitcase. "That's too heavy for you—here, let me take it."

Confusion ensues. Martha's right hand, the one crumpling the city map, lets go before Sonja's gotten a proper grip on the handle. The map flies away from them, it dances off, and the roll-along smacks against the tiles like a pistol shot.

Martha gives a start. *She's got some height to her*, thinks Sonja. *A little collapsed now, but when she was young she must have been decidedly tall.*

"Allow me," says Sonja, quickly bending over.

And it's there in an instant: the positional vertigo.

21.

A VAST EXCHANGE IS COMMENCING. Sonja can't claim otherwise; nobody can. It's barely visible yet, but it will be, and when it comes, it'll be vast.

"My sister had that too," Martha says.

They've found themselves a bench in Islands Brygge. The bench is handsomely designed and conceived for urban space, and the sun's sinking into thunderheads west of South Harbor. A darkness lies and lurks in the direction of Køge, but in the glow of sunset, Martha looks lovely and ancient. There are two of her, for Sonja's dizzy, but Martha's beauty isn't any the less for being twinned.

"She couldn't look up without everything going haywire. It started when she was about forty, and I don't know what triggered it, but I don't think she was very happy in her marriage. Not that she complained about it, but when we were at parties, she'd suddenly be sitting there strangely still, with her hands on her neck. It was those little stones."

"They have to settle into place," Sonja whispers. "They swirl around inside the ear, as if they're in flight and can't find their way out, and then you have to sit still till they come to terms with their situation. What did she do about it, your sister?"

Martha squints a little at the declining sun. Then she sighs and says she supposes her sister just learned to live with it.

"That's what one does, of course," Martha says. "You live with it, and you find your ways. I can recall one late summer when there was a huge meteor shower, and of course she wanted to see it. So we lay down in the grass and propped her up with pillows. She had an attack anyway, but I think we counted more than a hundred shooting stars that night."

She sits and flutters her fingertips against Sonja's hand, just like the clairvoyant chambermaid fluttered her fingers before her eye. The light touches feel like birds' feet on the back of Sonja's hand.

Then Sonja says, "But it doesn't matter. I manage, of course. It's mostly because I'm taking my driving test."

"In Copenhagen?" Martha asks, puzzled.

Where else? thinks Sonja, but she doesn't say that, because Martha's much too far from home to be able to handle Copenhagen irony.

"I took my test in Vinkel in 1965," Martha says. "There weren't any stoplights back then, so it was manageable."

"Are there stoplights there now?"

"Yes, one."

The heavy evening sun hangs over Valby Park like an orange. The late light lends the water a salmon cast, and the water plashes quietly as it laps against the quay wall. Now and then someone dashes by in tights, and there are tired bags under Martha's eyes. She's been a long time in transit, and it's a muggy evening, viscous and sticky, and everything that's supposed to get easier in life persists in being complicated;

Sonja can see that. *What kind of help am I going to be?* she thinks. *Me and my deficient sense of direction.*

"I'm going to sit here for a bit," Sonja says. "But the prime minister neighborhood is right in back of us if you're not afraid to strike out on your own. It's not that hard to find."

"Let's just sit here," says Martha.

"It's going to storm," says Sonja.

"It'll work out," says Martha, and then Sonja's no longer able to hold back the tears.

They well up from below, they force her mouth open and scrape the scales from her eyes, and now she is leaking, Martha fluttering, there's one stoplight in Vinkel, just one, and Sonja's mother would always say, "It'll all work out, it'll all work out."

"But sometimes," whispers Sonja, "things really don't work out. You see it all the time; how things don't work out at all. People suddenly maimed, broken, dead, and then things really didn't work out—or they did, they worked out terribly. And it's not supposed to happen that way, is it, that things work out terribly? Or that nothing you ever dreamed of comes to anything? The continents you wanted to explore turn out to be stripped of resources, drained and desolate. Stuntedness as far as the eye can see, and you know perfectly well that you should make the journey back to where you came from. That you have to change course and scrape yourself together, but how do you fool yourself that it was better in the place you left? The place you came from no longer exists, and I think I've lost the right to imagine my future."

Martha's hand flutters.

"I think you're just a little lonely."

"You better believe I am, and don't be ashamed about not being able to find Jens Otto Krag, for really it's me who's gotten lost," says Sonja, and she bends all the way forward while she weeps, yes, she's weeping, and the stones whirl round like a murmuration of starlings in her inner ears, they surge about and cast themselves quick here, quick there, they look like a fingerprint against the late summer sky. Then they swoop down over the rushes, swoop up over the rushes, they whoosh in across town and away from it again. They ought to land on the rooflines and form a black border against the sky, they ought to be singing with joy, yet for now they flit every which way, and Sonja flits with them in a silty blackness, a viscid underworld of sorrow and hands and then she's toppling off the bench, her face plunging toward the pavement except that Martha grabs her, she grabs hold of the back of Sonja's heart, or rather, she's grabbed hold of Sonja's bra strap and heaves her back up against the back of the bench.

"Goodness!" Martha says, but Sonja doesn't hear her because she's fainted.

In the realm she now haunts, they've seated themselves around the table. They're sitting in a large kitchen with home-baked bread. Mom goes around with brown sugar, maintaining equilibrium. Outside, the world is being subjected to violent transformation, and Sonja's happiness depends upon being able to adapt. "You're such a fighter," Mom says. "Kate can't cope, but you can," she says, and then a figure in a curry-colored tunic steps through the kitchen door. She walks discreetly over to the fridge and takes up a position there. "I can see a man with thinning hair," she says. "I can see that you will fall unhappily in love," and Sonja, who has lost her way out in the raging world and acquired jargons and behaviors to match, finds the situation comic—no, ironic, she finds it ironic. She isn't parrying the blows, and then the fortune teller says . . .

"Yes, what *did* the fortune teller say?" Sonja asks aloud.

She's raised her head upright, and Martha has her hand on Sonja's neck.

"You went all higgledy-piggledy there, didn't you?" Martha says, and now she's coming in clearer.

She takes on outline and contour; she wears a crinkly smile. The manner in which her hand supports Sonja's neck testifies to a kind of professionalism. *She has midwife's hands,* thinks Sonja. *She has hands that can gently and firmly bear baby to basin. Her eyes have peered into that which no one else knows. They're marked by a special form of insight. And loneliness.*

Somewhere in the distance, a blackbird sings in a solitary tree. Sonja can see the slats of the bench and the way Copenhagen keeps going nonstop on the other side of the canal. The attack is over. Sonja feels queasy, but no matter, for when the breeze touches it, she can feel that her face is moist.

"I think I'm going to give notice on my flat. One's always free to move, after all."

"Where will you go then?" asks Martha.

"Home."

"And your driver's license?"

"There is one stoplight in Vinkel," says Sonja. "But let's just sit here."

"Let's just sit here," says Martha.

"I hope you're not in a hurry," Sonja whispers.

"We're not going anywhere."

"The sun'll set soon."

"We've world enough and time," says Martha, and Sonja knows that, technically speaking, love requires more than a hand on the neck, but in the state she finds herself in, she loves Martha.

Yes, Sonja loves Martha.

Pushkin Press

Pushkin Press was founded in 1997, and publishes novels, essays, memoirs, children's books—everything from timeless classics to the urgent and contemporary.

Our books represent exciting, high-quality writing from around the world: we publish some of the twentieth century's most widely acclaimed, brilliant authors such as Stefan Zweig, Marcel Aymé, Teffi, Antal Szerb, Gaito Gazdanov and Yasushi Inoue, as well as compelling and award-winning contemporary writers, including Andrés Neuman, Edith Pearlman, Eka Kurniawan and Ayelet Gundar-Goshen.

Pushkin Press publishes the world's best stories, to be read and read again. Here are just some of the titles from our long and varied list. To discover more, visit www.pushkinpress.com.

THE SPECTRE OF ALEXANDER WOLF

GAITO GAZDANOV

'A mesmerising work of literature' Antony Beevor

SUMMER BEFORE THE DARK

VOLKER WEIDERMANN

'For such a slim book to convey with such poignancy the extinction of a generation of "Great Europeans" is a triumph' *Sunday Telegraph*

MESSAGES FROM A LOST WORLD

STEFAN ZWEIG

'At a time of monetary crisis and political disorder… Zweig's celebration of the brotherhood of peoples reminds us that there is another way' *The Nation*

BINOCULAR VISION

EDITH PEARLMAN

'A genius of the short story' Mark Lawson, *Guardian*

IN THE BEGINNING WAS THE SEA

TOMÁS GONZÁLEZ

'Smoothly intriguing narrative, with its touches of sinister, Patricia Highsmith-like menace' *Irish Times*

BEWARE OF PITY

STEFAN ZWEIG

'Zweig's fictional masterpiece' *Guardian*

THE ENCOUNTER

PETRU POPESCU

'A book that suggests new ways of looking at the world and our place within it' *Sunday Telegraph*

WAKE UP, SIR!

JONATHAN AMES

'The novel is extremely funny but it is also sad and poignant, and almost incredibly clever' *Guardian*

THE WORLD OF YESTERDAY

STEFAN ZWEIG

'*The World of Yesterday* is one of the greatest memoirs of the twentieth century, as perfect in its evocation of the world Zweig loved, as it is in its portrayal of how that world was destroyed' David Hare

WAKING LIONS

AYELET GUNDAR-GOSHEN

'A literary thriller that is used as a vehicle to explore big moral issues. I loved everything about it' *Daily Mail*

BONITA AVENUE

PETER BUWALDA

'One wild ride: a swirling helix of a family saga… a new writer as toe-curling as early Roth, as roomy as Franzen and as caustic as Houellebecq' *Sunday Telegraph*

JOURNEY BY MOONLIGHT

ANTAL SZERB

'Just divine… makes you imagine the author has had private access to your own soul' Nicholas Lezard, *Guardian*

BEFORE THE FEAST

SAŠA STANIŠIĆ

'Exceptional... cleverly done, and so mesmerising from the off... thought-provoking and energetic' *Big Issue*

A SIMPLE STORY

LEILA GUERRIERO

'An epic of noble proportions... [Guerriero] is a mistress of the telling phrase or the revealing detail' *Spectator*

FORTUNES OF FRANCE

ROBERT MERLE

1 *The Brethren*

2 *City of Wisdom and Blood*

3 *Heretic Dawn*

'Swashbuckling historical fiction' *Guardian*

TRAVELLER OF THE CENTURY

ANDRÉS NEUMAN

'A beautiful, accomplished novel: as ambitious as it is generous, as moving as it is smart' Juan Gabriel Vásquez, *Guardian*

ONE NIGHT, MARKOVITCH

AYELET GUNDAR-GOSHEN

'Wry, ironically tinged and poignant... this is a fable for the twenty-first century' *Sunday Telegraph*

KARATE CHOP & MINNA NEEDS REHEARSAL SPACE

DORTHE NORS

'Unique in form and effect... Nors has found a novel way of getting into the human heart' *Guardian*

RED LOVE: THE STORY OF AN EAST GERMAN FAMILY

MAXIM LEO

'Beautiful and supremely touching... an unbearably poignant description of a world that no longer exists' *Sunday Telegraph*

SONG FOR AN APPROACHING STORM

PETER FRÖBERG IDLING

'Beautifully evocative... a must-read novel' *Daily Mail*

THE RABBIT BACK LITERATURE SOCIETY

PASI ILMARI JÄÄSKELÄINEN

'Wonderfully knotty… a very grown-up fantasy masquerading as quirky fable. Unexpected, thrilling and absurd' *Sunday Telegraph*

STAMMERED SONGBOOK: A MOTHER'S BOOK OF HOURS

ERWIN MORTIER

'Mortier has a poet's eye for vibrant detail and prose to match… If this is a book of fragmentation, it is also a son's moving tribute' *Observer*

BARCELONA SHADOWS

MARC PASTOR

'As gruesome as it is gripping… the writing is extraordinarily vivid… Highly recommended' *Independent*

THE LIBRARIAN

MIKHAIL ELIZAROV

'A romping good tale… Pretty sensational' *Big Issue*

WHILE THE GODS WERE SLEEPING

ERWIN MORTIER

'A monumental, phenomenal book' *De Morgen*

BUTTERFLIES IN NOVEMBER

AUÐUR AVA ÓLAFSDÓTTIR

'A funny, moving and occasionally bizarre exploration of life's upheavals and reversals' *Financial Times*

BY BLOOD

ELLEN ULLMAN

'Delicious and intriguing' *Daily Telegraph*

THE LAST DAYS

LAURENT SEKSIK

'Mesmerising… Seksik's portrait of Zweig's final months is dignified and tender' *Financial Times*

TALKING TO OURSELVES

ANDRÉS NEUMAN

'This is writing of a quality rarely encountered… when you read Neuman's beautiful novel, you realise a very high bar has been set' *Guardian*